MaryJanice Davidson

"*Jennifer Scales and the Messenger of Light* is truly a wonderful read. Authors MaryJanice Davidson and Anthony Alongi have outdone themselves with this second of the series. Regardless of your age, this is one series which earns its place in any keeper shelf."

—*ParaNormal Romance Reviews*

"It's a great book whether you have read the other novel about Jennifer Scales or are new to the series. With an original, interesting plot, great writing, and awesome characters, *Jennifer Scales and the Messenger of Light* will resonate with teenagers—even if they don't change into spiders or dragons." —*Curled Up With a Good Kid's Book*

"A hilarious romp full of goofy twists and turns, great fun for fans of humorous vampire romance." —*Locus*

"Delightful, wicked fun!" —Christine Feehan

"One of the funniest, most satisfying series to come along lately. If you're fans of Sookie Stackhouse and Anita Blake, don't miss Betsy Taylor. She rocks." —*The Best Reviews*

Berkley Sensation titles by MaryJanice Davidson

UNDEAD AND UNPOPULAR
UNDEAD AND UNRETURNABLE
UNDEAD AND UNAPPRECIATED
UNDEAD AND UNEMPLOYED
UNDEAD AND UNWED

DEAD AND LOVING IT

DERIK'S BANE

Jove titles by MaryJanice Davidson

SLEEPING WITH THE FISHES

Titles by MaryJanice Davidson and Anthony Alongi

JENNIFER SCALES AND THE ANCIENT FURNACE
JENNIFER SCALES AND THE MESSENGER OF LIGHT

Jennifer Scales

and the

Ancient Furnace

*MaryJanice Davidson
and
Anthony Alongi*

ACE BOOKS, NEW YORK

THE BERKLEY PUBLISHING GROUP
Published by the Penguin Group
Penguin Group (USA) Inc.
375 Hudson Street, New York, New York 10014, USA
Penguin Group (Canada), 90 Eglinton Avenue East, Suite 700, Toronto, Ontario M4P 2Y3, Canada
(a division of Pearson Penguin Canada Inc.)
Penguin Books Ltd., 80 Strand, London WC2R 0RL, England
Penguin Group Ireland, 25 St. Stephen's Green, Dublin 2, Ireland (a division of Penguin Books Ltd.)
Penguin Group (Australia), 250 Camberwell Road, Camberwell, Victoria 3124, Australia
(a division of Pearson Australia Group Pty. Ltd.)
Penguin Books India Pvt. Ltd., 11 Community Centre, Panchsheel Park, New Delhi—110 017, India
Penguin Group (NZ), Cnr. Airborne and Rosedale Roads, Albany, Auckland 1310, New Zealand
(a division of Pearson New Zealand Ltd.)
Penguin Books (South Africa) (Pty.) Ltd., 24 Sturdee Avenue, Rosebank, Johannesburg 2196,
South Africa

Penguin Books Ltd., Registered Offices: 80 Strand, London WC2R 0RL, England

This is a work of fiction. Names, characters, places, and incidents either are the product of the authors' imagination or are used fictitiously, and any resemblance to actual persons, living or dead, business establishments, events, or locales is entirely coincidental. The publisher does not have any control over and does not assume any responsibility for author or third-party websites or their content.

JENNIFER SCALES AND THE ANCIENT FURNACE

An Ace Book / published by arrangement with the authors

PRINTING HISTORY
Berkley Jam trade paperback edition / August 2005
Ace mass-market edition / February 2007

Copyright © 2005 by MaryJanice Davidson Alongi and Anthony Alongi.
Cover art by Jerry Vanderstelt.
Cover design by Lesley Worrell.
Interior text design by Stacy Irwin.

ISBN: 978-0-441-01474-3

ACE
Ace Books are published by The Berkley Publishing Group,
a division of Penguin Group (USA) Inc.,
375 Hudson Street, New York, New York 10014.
ACE and the "A" design are trademarks belonging to Penguin Group (USA) Inc.

PRINTED IN THE UNITED STATES OF AMERICA

10 9 8 7 6 5 4 3 2 1

For the daughters:
Gabriela Alongi, Christina Alongi, and Erika Growette,
whose help was invaluable

PROLOGUE

The Ruin of Eveningstar

On the day Jennifer Scales turned five, her family was forced to move. It was the morning their quiet river town of Eveningstar, Minnesota, died a horrible death.

Jennifer remembered only dim dawn light against her window, her mother rousing her, and jeans and a sweatshirt finding their way onto her tired body while her head drooped against her chest.

If she thought a little harder, she could remember walking through the crisp, brown woods behind her house until they reached the Mississippi River, stepping onto a flat, slippery boat that sunk a bit with her weight, and shivering in her mother's firm arms while her father's voice calmly reassured her.

And if she relaxed her mind, which she wouldn't be able to do until she was older, she could remember standing on a bluff beyond the other side of the river, watching from a safe distance as her hometown burned *under a crescent moon. She heard the roars of beasts—dinosaurs?—the howls of wolves, and the screeches of unknown things.*

The morning of September 18, those things laid waste to Eveningstar. No one from beyond its borders ever tried to put out the fires, or bury those who died there, or even report the incident.

No one went there. No one remembered there. Eveningstar, Minnesota, settled by Scandinavian immigrants and incorporated more than one hundred years past, fell into ashes and out of existence.

CHAPTER 1

The Flip

The Winoka Falcons were on the verge of their third straight Community Junior League Soccer Championship. In sudden-death overtime, the score was tied at 1–1 with the Northwater Shooting Stars. Jennifer Scales, the Falcons captain, dribbled the ball across midfield. Four of her teammates charged forward with her; only three exhausted defenders were keeping pace.

Jennifer, who had turned fourteen the day before, wanted a win for her birthday present.

As one of the Northwater defenders approached, she kicked the ball sharply to the left, into what could have been open field. It skimmed the grass and nestled squarely in the instep of her teammate, Susan Elmsmith. Jennifer grinned in delight at her friend's sudden change in pace and direction. There were times she was sure the two of them could read each other's mind.

Susan advanced on the enemy net with gritted teeth.

Jennifer slipped behind the defender who had challenged her and matched pace with the last opposing fullback, being careful not to slip offsides.

Unfortunately, it had rained most of yesterday, and though the skies were clear today, the ground was treacherous. More than twenty yards away from the goal, Susan went skidding into the grass and mud with an angry yell, just managing to push the ball a bit off the ground and over the foot of the fullback. It came spinning by Jennifer, and in a tenth of a second she saw her shot.

She darted forward and kicked the ball straight up with her toe. Then she somersaulted into the air, twisted, and sent the ball sailing toward the net with a hard kick. For an upside-down instant she saw the goalie dangling in the sky from the earth above. Then she twisted again, completed the midair roll, and landed on her feet as the ball flew past the goalie's reaching fingers.

Game over, 2–1, Falcons.

She turned back downfield grinning, already anticipating the slaps and congratulations from her teammates. But all the players on the field were staring at her in surprise, and a little bit of . . . fear?

"How did you do that?" Susan's eyes, usually almond-shaped, were wide with shock. "You turned upside down . . . It was so *fast*."

"Duh, it had to be," Jennifer shot back. They were gaping at her as if she'd pulled a second head out of her butt and kicked *that* into the net. "Jeez, any of you could have done it. I was just closest to the ball."

"No," Terry Fox, another teammate, said. Her voice sounded strange and thin. "We couldn't have."

Then the field was crowded with parents from the stands, and their ecstatic coach, who lifted Jennifer by the elbows and shook her like a maraca. She forgot about the odd reactions of her friends and reveled in the win.

In all the ruckus, she didn't think to look at her mother's reaction to her stunt. By the time she sought her out in the crowd, the older woman was cheering and clapping like everyone else.

Winoka was a town where autumn wanted to last longer, but found itself squeezed out by the legendary Minnesota winters. Like many suburbs, it had new middle-class neighborhoods built on top of old farmland and inside small forests. The Scales's house, at 9691 Pine Street East, was in one of those lightly forested neighborhoods, where every house had a three-car garage, ivy-stone walls, and a mobile basketball net on the edge of a neatly manicured lawn. It looked incredibly typical. Jennifer could never figure out why this bothered her.

The night of the championship, however, she wasn't thinking about the house. She was thinking about her friends. She wanted her mother to think about them, too.

"Freaking out! Acting like I had sprouted wings!"

Dr. Elizabeth Georges-Scales was a woman who didn't often show emotion. If her daughter had been paying close attention, though, she might have noticed a slight pull at the edges of her solemn eyes.

"When the coach took us out for ice cream afterward, everyone seemed cool," Jennifer continued. "But I still caught Chris and Terry staring at me when they thought I wasn't looking."

"It was quite a jump," Elizabeth offered mildly.

"I see players on the U.S. team do it all the time."

"Really."

Jennifer hissed softly. If the older woman wasn't looking right at her, Jennifer would swear she didn't have her mother's attention at all. Typical! A vague and absent look, meaningless verbal agreement, and no maternal instincts whatsoever.

Did you actually give birth to me, or did you just crack open a test tube? She did not say this aloud. The rush she'd get from forcing a reaction from her mother was not worth the weekend grounding she'd receive.

Besides, she had to give her mother credit for being at the game today—and every other soccer game Jennifer had ever played. And this was one of their longest conversations in weeks.

So Jennifer passed on the insult. "They were weird, is all I'm saying. High school just started, I'm under enough pressure . . . now this!" The ringing doorbell jerked them both out of the conversation. "I'll get it." She grabbed cash from her mother's hand and answered the door.

The delivery guy was tall, blond, wiry, and unfortunately plagued by enough acne to cover twelve boys his size. "H-have a nice s-supper," he stuttered after passing her the bags of food. He wouldn't stop staring, so she finally stuffed some cash in his shirt pocket and shut the door on him.

It was her eyes, probably. Sometimes boys stared at her eyes. They were a shining gray—almost silver—and seemed to cast their own light. Her father had similar eyes, and grown women stared at *him* as much as gangly boys stared at *her*. The idea of her dad as a babe magnet grossed her out, but her mom never seemed to notice.

"My!" Jennifer said, spreading out the delivered feast. Lemon chicken and pork spareribs for her, beef lo mein and potstickers for her mother, white rice, about a thousand tiny soy sauce packets, and factory-wrapped fortune cookies for both of them. "What a delicious meal, Mother. How do you find the time?"

"Very funny." Elizabeth smirked. "You know perfectly well neither of us wants me to cook."

Jennifer grinned back, glad of the momentary connection. "True, true. Hey, some stuff you cook is really great. For example, your eggs. And your, uh, soup. Your soup is the best."

"I'll tell the Campbell's Corporation you said so." Elizabeth was really smiling, now. It didn't happen often, and Jennifer observed how young her mother looked.

She usually preferred not to notice. She had once overheard a couple of boys in her eighth-grade class who had been to her house. The way they talked about her mother made Jennifer uncomfortable, to say the least.

Height seemed to be the draw. Height made legs longer, inexplicably made shoulder-length honey-blonde hair shinier, even cheekbones higher. It somehow made emerald eyes sharper, and smoothed out the pronounced curves from bearing a child. And this tall frame moved with a sort of direct grace that didn't remind Jennifer so much of a medical doctor as a gymnast.

By comparison, Jennifer felt inadequate. While her mother's height made her beautiful, Jennifer's made her feel like a misfit. The only place she felt at home was on the soccer field, where everybody was yards away from each other and nobody had time to compare your body to everyone else's. In the crowded hallways of Winoka High, in front of every boy and girl she knew (and many she didn't), her height and eyes stood out, her loud laugh stood out, and the silver streaks that had just shown up in her blonde hair this year *definitely* stood out.

The hair really bothered her. While her father had pointed out that the emerging color matched her eyes, she could not stand that her hair had begun to turn "old-lady gray" before she even turned fourteen. First she had tried dye, but the silver strands never seemed to hold the color. Then she considered wigs, but she felt ridiculous the first time she tried one on in a store—and of course, she knew a wig would never work on a soccer field. Nowadays, she just wore simple hats whenever she could. Threads of silver always seemed to wriggle out from under the brim.

Sometimes, when she looked in the mirror, Jennifer thought she looked like an older version of her mother.

The aroma of the lemon chicken chased away uncomfortable thoughts, and she began to eat.

"Your dad's coming home tonight," Elizabeth offered between bites of lo mein.

"Really." The mention of her father irritated Jennifer. "Seems soon."

"It's been five days," her mother pointed out.

"Like clockwork, I guess."

"Perhaps you could show him that soccer trick."

Jennifer let her fork fall loudly. "If he wanted to see it, he could have been at the game."

"You know he goes when he can."

"I know he goes on another business trip to nowhere, once or twice a month, and I never know if he's going to be there or not."

"It's his job."

"I thought being my father was also his job. It was the championship game."

"He didn't have a choice."

"Sure he did. Every time he flies off on another trip, he has to move his own feet and step onto a plane."

There was a pause. "It's not like that."

Jennifer pushed away the chicken. "I hate that you think it's no big deal."

Elizabeth pushed her own meal away. "Jennifer, honestly. When he's around, all you do is tell him how irritating he is. Then he leaves, and you complain that he's not around."

"I'm sorry I can't be a rational, emotionless robot like you, Mom. Cripes. Why can't *you* be the one that leaves every couple weeks?"

Jennifer immediately saw from her mother's startled reaction that she had crossed over several lines way too fast. She hadn't meant the conversation to go like this. It had seemed so pleasant just a minute ago.

Before she could muster the will to apologize, her mother was up from the dinner table and dumping the rest of her dinner into the dog dish. Phoebe, a collie-shepherd mix with enormous black, pointed ears, came racing out of the living room at the sound of food hitting her bowl. Just like that, Phoebe was in the kitchen and her mother wasn't.

By the time Jonathan Scales got home that evening, his daughter had immersed herself in charcoal sketches. Piles of chalky black-and-white drafts of angels, dragons, and faeries littered the floor of Jennifer's bedroom. As he edged open the door, he pushed some aside.

"Hey, ace. Drawing up a storm? How'd the game go?"

Jennifer fixed her eyes on his. "For someone who claims to be my father, you do an amazing impersonation of someone who doesn't know *anything* about *anyone* else around here."

Jonathan sighed and closed the door.

* * *

Later that night, Jennifer and her mother were talking over leftovers. They were both smiling this time, but then suddenly Jennifer changed. She could feel her skin *moving,* and her face stretching. Glancing down at her hands, Jennifer saw the backs of them turn electric blue, and her fingernails grow rapidly and thicken. When she looked back up, her mother was staring at her—not with surprise or fear, but with calm hatred. The older woman's features were dark and horrible. Her mortal enemy.

With lightning reflexes, she surged over the kitchen table, opened her jaws, and bit her mother's head cleanly off with a bloody snap.

Then she woke up.

"So perhaps you could explain why you did that," her father said. They were all in the kitchen the next morning, Saturday, eating breakfast. A chill autumn wind swung through the half-open window above the sink.

Jennifer had not said a word all morning. She was staring at her mother, who was sitting exactly where she had been during dinner, and in her dream. Elizabeth looked nothing like the vision of hatred and danger from the dream. Instead, she was pale, with her hair in a tortured mess.

Jennifer stole a look at her hands.

Still pink. And the fingernails were still short.

She tried to calm down. Her bad dream meant nothing beyond some guilt.

Speaking of which.

"Jennifer?" Her father's irritation caught her attention.

"I'm sorry," she offered kindly enough to her mother. "I lost my temper last night."

There was no anger in Elizabeth's eyes, just a hollow kind of sadness pulling lines of age tighter under the brows. Jennifer felt a knot tighten at the bottom of her throat. She chewed her tongue nervously.

"Really, Mom . . . I'm sorry."

Her eyes did not change. "You should show your father how you won the game yesterday."

Jennifer wondered at the change of subject but was glad enough of it. If her mother wanted to sweep this under the rug, fine. She shrugged and shoved her chair back. "Let's go outside, Dad."

"Hold on." For a moment, Jennifer was certain that he would not honor the get-out-of-argument-free pass his wife had just offered. But instead of frowning, he pointed thoughtfully at the bowl of oranges on the table. "Toss me a couple of those oranges."

Jennifer picked two—she was sure he couldn't be thinking what *she* thought he might be thinking, was he?—and lobbed them to her father. Then she backed up into the open space by the patio door. The kitchen was large, but she had never really thought about jumping and flipping in here. The tile felt suddenly cold and slippery under her bare feet. "Right here?"

"Yep. Your target is the TV."

With the patio door to her back, she turned her head left and looked through the large archway into the family room. The black screen of the forty-inch television at the far end reflected her surprised expression. "Dad, this is weird. Why don't we just—"

"We can do it right here and forget about the awful things you said to your mother last night. Or we can go outside, which will be the last time you feel the sun shine on your face until next spring." Her father said this in a perfectly pleasant, uniquely terrifying tone.

"Right." She cleared her throat and crouched down a bit onto the balls of her feet. "Oranges away."

He shifted one orange into his left hand and lobbed it gently underhand, over the table, and a bit too high.

Jennifer shifted her weight to her left foot, skipped a quarter step back, and sprang. The kitchen pitched about her—there was that old water stain in the corner of the ceiling—and she twisted in time to slam her foot into the orange, hurtling it into the living room. She heard a dull thud and landed firmly with her toes back on the tiles.

The fruit had impaled itself on the upper left corner of the mahogany television frame. Juice and seeds were dribbling down onto the eggshell carpet.

"Off the bar," her father said with a smile. "Close, but no goal. Try again."

This was silly. Jennifer looked to her mother for help. There was none there. "Fine. Keep 'em coming, as fast as you like. I'll kick the whole bowl of Florida goodness into the television, if that's what you want."

"Yes, you will. Make sure you get each one."

Another orange went into the air. Jennifer watched it as it came in a bit lower than the first, and to her left. She quickly adjusted and flipped into the air again.

Halfway through the flip, she saw to her annoyance that her father had thrown another orange up after the first. She completed the kick and landed, then darted two steps forward to manage this new target. From the living room, she could hear the smash of glass as the first missile met its mark.

Undistracted, she twirled up to the second and . . . saw a third orange, which her father apparently had sent after the second one. *Jerk,* she hissed to herself, and resolved to send the second orange into a different piece of expensive entertainment equipment. *The stereo system would do nicely.* With a clean *thwack* her long foot sent the citrus rocket cruising higher than the last one.

She came down in plenty of time to adjust to the third, which was lower and close to her original position. *Testing me,* she guessed, and therefore decided upon the lamp on the end table to the left of the living room couch.

A moment later, she was back on her feet. The living room was a disaster—a shattered lamp, a cracked digital display on the stereo amplifier, and a television set that desperately needed a new cathode tube. The cloying odor of oranges filled the air.

She surveyed the devastation with satisfaction, and then looked at her parents. They had the oddest faces.

"What?" she asked, a bit crossly. "You told me to kick the darn oranges, so I kicked them. I'm sorry I hit the other stuff, but what was with throwing three oranges one right after the other like that?"

"Your father did throw three oranges . . ." admitted her mother, in a very slow and measured tone.

Jennifer looked at her father. Jonathan Scales did not say a word. She had almost never seen him this afraid, not like this, not since she chased a kickball into the street in front of a car when she was eight.

Her mother went on. ". . . But he didn't throw the oranges one at a time. He threw them all at once."

They all stared at each other for a few seconds. When her father finally said something, it was not at all what Jennifer expected.

"It's coming faster than we thought," he whispered, more to himself than anyone else.

After being exiled gently but firmly to her room, Jennifer could not hear much of the conversation that followed downstairs. But that didn't stop her from trying.

Coming faster? What's *coming faster? The oranges?*

She heard snippets and phrases—"rapid change" and "crescent moon" came up—but her parents were not careless enough to speak above harsh whispers.

After a few minutes of this, she began to feel resentful. Why were they talking about her, without her in the room, when they knew she was just upstairs? Wasn't this about her? Wasn't this *her* life?

A rap at her window startled her. She guessed who it was before she turned to look; only Susan was both daring and nimble enough to climb the slippery trellis on the outside wall. Indeed it was her best friend's cascading black hair, bright blue eyes, and genuine smile on the other side of the glass. Jennifer crossed her room and lifted the lower pane.

"Hey, Flipper! Bounce any balls off your tail, lately?"

"Ha-ha. I have laughed. What are you doing here?" Jennifer was relieved to hear her friend making light of the kick everyone had found so strange yesterday.

"Bunch of us are going out to Terry's farm today, do up a bonfire, roast some apples and stuff. You coming?"

Jennifer's shoulders sagged. "I don't know. Mom and Dad are freaking out on me; I'll probably be stuck here for a while. How long will you be?"

"Just a few hours. We might go to the movies after,

though." Some brown curls lifted gently by the breeze floated through the window as Susan tilted her head. "Your parents are freaking out, huh? About that kick?"

"I suppose."

"What, they think you're on drugs?"

"I don't think so." Jennifer sat down on her bed. "They're whispering weird stuff about something coming."

Her friend giggled. "Puberty?"

"Ugh, grow up! No, something else. I have no idea. I've never seen them like this. Normally, they don't seem to care *what* I do."

Susan was suddenly thoughtful. "Um, you're not *actually*...? I mean, you're weren't *on* anything during the..."

Jennifer stopped her with a raised hand. "Don't start on me. I'm so *not* in the mood for this."

"You gotta admit, you've never done anything like that before. I mean, you're the best player on our team and all, but... you should have seen yourself. You looked totally juiced up."

"So, what? You're saying I *am* on drugs, and you don't believe me?" She could feel her own face getting red. Susan was probably right—this is what her parents were muttering about! They were going to ground her! For *drugs!* This was so unfair!

Her friend shifted uncomfortably on the trellis. "Geez, Jenny, don't have a heart attack. I'm just saying people aren't going to know what happened. They're going to think it's strange."

"You mean *I'm* strange. And don't call me Jenny."

"I didn't say *you* were strange. And since when do you care if *I* call you Jenny?"

"I was 'Jenny' when I was six years old. I'm in high school now and I like 'Jennifer' better. And wouldn't I *have* to be strange? Isn't everyone just saying I'm a freak, slipping steroids or whatever?"

Susan looked down at the ground below. "Listen, Jen, I gotta go. Are you coming or not?"

"Yeah, sure, right after I pop my pills and shoot up."

"Fine. I'm out of here." Without even looking back up, Susan scrambled swiftly down the trellis and was gone.

Jennifer seethed as she stared out the open window for a moment, then got up and slammed it shut. She crossed her room, whipped open the door, and shouted down the stairs to her whispering parents.

"I'm not on drugs!"

CHAPTER 2

Screaming Butterflies

It was a wretched few weeks after that. While her parents released her from her room after an hour that day, they didn't say much more about oranges, or drugs, or what was "coming," or anything else. Her father seemed on several occasions to want to say something, but at the last moment, he would just sigh and mutter about how he was always available if she needed someone to listen.

Of course, he went off on another trip for five days.

Meanwhile, Jennifer continued to have disturbing dreams. In some, she was a dinosaur attacking her parents. In others, she was an angel drowning in the clouds. In still others, she was a python in the dark, coiled around a tree branch and waiting to drop onto her friends.

All of this was too unsettling to share. So she just lurked around the house, waiting for her parents to say something, and wishing they wouldn't. And while Susan and the rest of the soccer team weren't nasty to her, they weren't exactly friendly either. Fixing relationships there would take time.

About two weeks after the day with the oranges, she barged bravely through the front doors of the still-frightening high school and nearly ran over Edward Blacktooth. And she smiled for the first time in what felt like a year.

Eddie, her next-door neighbor, reminded her of a sparrow. He had pale skin and deep brown accents in his hair and eyes, and his nose arced like a gentle beak. A crooked, mischievous smile graced his face as he and Jennifer recognized each other.

"Eddie!" she cried, delighted. "You're back!"

"Jenny!" He grinned. He knew she hated that nickname. "The soccer star who rules the school. They haven't skipped you up to tenth grade yet?"

"Hardly." She blushed. "How was England?"

Normally Eddie started the school year with everyone else, but this year his family had insisted on taking him on some strange month-long vacation in England. Eddie had told Jennifer before leaving that they would visit ancient churches, museums, fortresses, and other horrifically boring historical points of supposed interest. Apparently, he could trace his ancestry back several centuries to some baron who lived in a castle not far from Wales.

"The castle was pretty interesting. Everything else was tolerable. We had a good time—Mom and Dad even smiled once or twice. How goes the battle?" Eddie was always talking in military metaphors: How goes the battle? Who's winning the war? What an amazing coup!

"The battle goes badly," she muttered as he fell into step beside her. "Way badly."

"Oh, don't let people like her get you down."

She looked at him. Brown T-shirt and blue jeans. Brown loafers. His mud-colored hair fell into his eyes and he flicked it back with a jerk of his head. And for the first time, Jennifer noticed a faint scent of aftershave. Edward Blacktooth was reliable, there when you needed him, less so when you didn't. He was—Eddie. "People like who?" she asked.

He breathed in a bit and then spoke quickly. "Nothing against Susan. The three of us have been buds since first grade. But I heard about that kick, and she's obviously jealous. You two have owned the soccer field together for a long time. Next year, when you both try out for the varsity team, she'll have to start at the bottom again—but maybe you won't. She sees that and doesn't like it."

Jennifer didn't answer right away. Eddie pressed.

"It's her problem, Jen. She'll deal with it herself."

She nodded and tried to smile. True, Eddie could be a bit of a snob—he got that from his parents, who disliked everybody—and Susan was deeper than Eddie let on. But right now, Jennifer didn't care. She knew why he said those things.

"Thanks, Eddie."

"Welcome. See you in gym." He casually smacked her shoulder and took a sharp left. She stared after him for a long moment, then started walking to class.

"Everyone, this is Francis—"

"Skip."

Ms. Graf squinted at the yellow transfer sheet. "Francis Wilson."

"Please, just Skip," the new kid sighed. Jennifer fought down a giggle. Skip Wilson's eyes were green, or maybe blue, set far apart from a narrow nose and under dark chocolate hair. He was taller than Ms. Graf, who many students dubbed "Ms. Giraffe," and his incredibly long fingers splayed across his schoolbook: *Principles and Applications of Calculus.*

In ninth grade? She thought to herself. She had felt pretty bright for picking up Advanced Algebra this year.

"Skip's family just moved here to Winoka from out of state, right, Skip?"

He shrugged.

Ms. Graf was a veteran teacher and knew to give up at that point. "Just have a seat right there," she said, pointing to the empty desk behind Jennifer.

The silence in the classroom was pronounced. Jennifer felt sorry for this boy. This was, after all, high school. No one was going to say hello, or smile, or even really look at him. No one ever did.

Except for Bob Jarkmand. As Skip walked between him and Jennifer, Bob stuck out his enormous leg.

The heavy and thick limb was squarely in the new kid's way. Jennifer sighed. This was one of the moments when being a girl was definitely better than the alternative. When Skip tried to step over it, Bob would bring his leg up and kick him in the groin. He would then feign innocence while his victim doubled over in pain. Then Ms. Graf would try to figure out what had happened, and everyone would be too scared of Bob to speak up. Then the bell would ring and they'd all forget about it. Except for the new kid, who would never feel more alone and friendless in his entire life.

Jennifer watched, wondering whether to intervene.

Bob reserved his worst bullying for boys, and generally ignored girls unless he felt like making a crude remark about breasts or bodily functions to get his cronies laughing. Another day, she would not have hesitated to speak up—but today, she wasn't sure she needed the additional aggravation, just to help some new kid who may turn out to be a jerk himself.

She had no time to resolve the issue. Skip raised his leg to step over Bob's leg, and then—just as the larger boy's leg kicked—jumped straight up in the air, outperforming Bob's knee by at least six inches. At the same time, he swung his heavy textbook around, catching Bob in the side of the head so hard, everyone in class looked up at the sound.

But by then, Skip was sliding into the seat behind Jennifer, and Bob was bellowing like a walrus. It had all happened so fast, she was certain no one else saw it. She stared, mouth open in delight.

Bob's ear was an angry red and was already swelling. He spun his head around and spat at Skip.

"You're dead, *Francis!*"

Skip turned in his seat—eyes, head, and body in full—to face the other boy. Jen was impressed with how calm the new boy seemed.

"I don't see that happening," he replied.

Ms. Graf, of course, had missed the entire thing. She was pulling a stack of large, wooden picture frames off of a low shelf behind her desk.

"Today, class, we will start our unit on insects. We begin with the order *lepidoptera* . . . more commonly known as butterflies and moths. *Lepidoptera* means, literally, 'scaled wings.'"

Jennifer perked up a bit at that. Scaled wings—that

sounded kind of cool. And she'd always thought insects were fascinating. When she was younger, she'd catch dragonflies and grasshoppers and butterflies with her bare hands and look at their heads through a magnifying glass. They had the sweetest expressions.

Sadly, Ms. Graf could render even the most interesting subject lifeless. Within ten minutes Jennifer had gone from clear-eyed interest to droopy-eyed boredom. Next to her, Bob had tilted his head and begun snoring.

She came all the way awake when Ms. Graf opened the picture frame cases and began taking out specimens.

"Of course," the teacher said, "there's nothing like seeing these creatures up close to get a full sense of their beauty, complexity, and elegance."

Small cards made their way from the front of the class to the back. Touch gently, they were told.

Pinned to the center of the first yellowed three-by-five index card was a gorgeous monarch butterfly. Its orange-black whorls strained against the paper, and its body was half-decomposed.

The metal spikes driven through its soft, scaled wings seemed incredibly cruel to Jennifer. Wincing, she chucked the card behind her.

"Whoa, hey, easy!" the new kid mumbled as he tried to catch the ungainly missile. "Lessee . . . mmmm . . . lunch."

She allowed a giggle at the remark, and at her own squeamish reaction, even while her stomach tightened with nausea. Or was it empathy? Why the heck would she care so much about some dumb bugs on cards?

Another card came back—a rusty red butterfly, with four bright blue spots at the corners of its wings. Black, yellow, and white markings graced the spots.

She flipped the card. On the back, in neat pencil, were the words: *Peacock Butterfly. Inachis io. Ireland.* One of the pins lanced the top loop of the "B." Jennifer winced again, and turned the card back over to look at the poor thing.

The four bluish markings stared back at her, like lidless eyes. Jennifer paused. There was something scary about this. She couldn't place it. It was an instinct, or a warning of danger . . .

A sharp poke on her right shoulder made her flinch. *Attack!* She whipped her left hand up and grabbed . . . the new kid's finger.

"Hey," Skip muttered with a crooked smile. "Easy, champ. I just wondered if I could look at the next one. And, um, maybe have my finger back?"

Jennifer relaxed, flashed an easy smile, let go of his finger, and handed back the peacock butterfly. "Sorry. Don't poke me."

"Sorry. Nice reflexes."

Jennifer felt red around her ears. "Thanks."

The penciled script on the back of the next card listed *Five Bar Swordtail. Pathysa antiphates. Singapore.* The Swordtail was an elegant thing, with black and green stripes painting the length of its wings, accented with yellow and white midwing markings.

Suddenly, it screamed.

"Cripes!" shrieked Jennifer, dropping the wailing butterfly onto her lap. This made the screeching worse. She darted out of her chair, letting the card flap onto the floor, and backed up several paces.

"Ms. Scales!" Ms. Graf fixed her with astonished eyes. "What is the matter?"

Jennifer looked back down at the butterfly. Its wings

were pulling against the pins in vain. It stopped screaming long enough to pant for a piece, but then started right
up again.

The stares of her classmates and Ms. Graf gave her
more information than she wanted. She pointed down at
the screeching Swordtail. "No one else hears that?"

Ms. Graf sighed. "Ninth graders are never as funny as
they think. Ms. Scales, please take your seat."

Bob Jarkmand guffawed. Jennifer wasn't sure if he was
laughing at her, or with her. It did seem from the smirks at
other desks as though most of the class felt she was playing a prank. She smiled uneasily, accepting the praise for
breaking a school day's tedium, and sat back down.

Another poke at her right shoulder. "Um, if you're
sure that's dead, could you pass it on back?"

Jennifer heard herself hiss. This boy Skip was lovably
weird, perhaps, but also a bit of a pain. And hadn't she
told him to stop poking her? "Give me a sec."

She bent over and picked up the card. The butterfly
was sobbing now.

It was awful. Jennifer felt like she was a conspirator in
the plot to hurt this thing. She turned to the tall classroom
windows—shut against the chilly October morning—that
provided a view of the nearby farms. She wanted to burst
out of her chair, yank one of the windows open, pull the
pins out of the card, and set this creature free.

Skip's voice behind her broke her thought. "Ummm . . ."

"In a minute." She was certain this boy irritated her
now. A pity Bob hadn't managed to rack the nimble pest!

The butterfly's peals of pain and sorrow went on. She
looked back at the classroom windows. What was she
thinking? Everyone would laugh at her. And what was
the big deal anyway? Despite what her ears told her, this

butterfly was dead. It wasn't going to come back from the dead and haunt her like a little buggy ghost.

There was no outcry in its murdered sleep, no appeal for revenge, no family to care whether it lived or died . . .

Pleck.

A spot appeared on one of the windows. Jennifer squinted to make out the shape. A rather large bug had run into the glass and splattered itself.

Pleck. Pleck.

Two more spots appeared, right near the first. Jennifer could make out long, transparent wings on the remains. It was getting dark outside.

Pleck-pleck. Pleck-pleck-pleck. Pleck-pleck.

Like sharp drops of rain, more small, smooth bodies dashed themselves against the gloomy windows. Dragonflies, Jennifer saw now. Underneath the rhythm, she could make out a low, thrilling hum.

"Um, Ms. Graf?" One of the girls close to the window had noticed the bugs, too.

Before the teacher could react, a barrage of dragonflies drove themselves into the window. Heedless of their fate, they landed with the force and volume of hailstones. Cracks began to appear in the glass.

"Everybody out of the room!"

Nobody moved. It was too terrifying. The hairline cracks lengthened and connected to each other. A chip of glass fell onto the countertop below. Still the black swarm came. It was even larger farther out in the sky, where it blotted out the sun. A vast column was aimed like a twister at the southeast corner of Winoka High's second floor.

In the midst of the chaos, Jennifer stole a glance at the Swordtail. It wailed in her hands. Her gut churned.

"Stop it," she whispered to it. The butterfly ignored her. *"Stop it!"*

It stopped.

The dragonflies vanished. Not the dead ones—those still stuck like wretched paste all over the classroom windows. But the humming and splattering stopped, and the cloud outside dissipated.

Jennifer turned around slowly, and let the butterfly drop onto Skip's desk. Like everyone else, he was looking at the windows—no one had noticed Jennifer's whispered command to the butterfly. But his face was aglow.

"That was *cool!*"

Jennifer knew better than to bring the matter up with her parents. But the moment she got home from school, she discovered it was useless to hide anything.

"I heard about the dragonflies," her father said as she walked by the kitchen table where he and her mother were sitting.

"Fine, thanks, and you?"

"Jennifer, I think we need to talk. Before I go on my trip tonight."

"Why yes, Father, my day *was* nice. And yours?"

"Now, Jennifer."

"Daa-aad!" She stomped her foot. "I don't want to talk about this. It was a bunch of dumb dragonflies. Tonight, on the news, they'll say it was a tornado. Or a weather balloon. Who knows? Who cares?"

"We don't want to talk about the dragonflies. We want to talk about you, and changes that are coming."

"You've got to be kidding. Even *you* can't be this clueless. I learned that stuff in third grade. You gave me books. I surfed the Internet. Boy loves girl, girl loves . . ."

"Oh for heaven's sake, Jennifer, be quiet," hissed Elizabeth.

She stared at her mother. Elizabeth Georges-Scales was holding her head in her hands. Tears were streaking down the doctor's cheeks. Jennifer felt tears well up in her own eyes. If she didn't know better, she would have thought someone had died. "What—what's wrong?"

"Sit down, ace." Her father kicked out a chair. "There's no easy way through this."

Two hours later, sobbing into her pillow up in her own room, Jennifer had to agree with at least *that* much. There was no easy way, not at all, anymore.

CHAPTER 3

The Crescent Moon

Mors vestra gloria nostra erit. *Your death is our glory.*

"My—what?" Jennifer looked around her. She was in a dark, cold place, and it hurt to move. "My death?"

Justice. Law. Prophecy. You die, worm.

"What is this place? Who are you?"

A small fire burst in front of her eyes. Ms. Graf stepped out of the flames. Gone were the glasses and frumpy dress: She was in full shining armor with a glittering crown on her head. "It doesn't matter. You're leaving now." There was the whisper of a blade leaving its sheath, the song of the sword slicing through the air, and then the greatest agony Jennifer had ever known. She reached out, too little too late. The room tipped crazily and she rolled toward the fire. Her body stood still behind her. It was the body of a Swordtail butterfly, with bent wings and no head. Then it toppled over backward . . .

* * *

Jennifer sat bolt upright in her bed. The faint edge of sunset warmed the room. Her hands flew to her neck, making sure her head was still there.

Bad enough she was a freak, bad enough her parents had gone crazy, but these nightmares were getting out of hand.

She looked at the time. The early autumn darkness had fooled her; it was only six o'clock. It was Friday night, her friends were probably at the mall, and she was here in her room, sulking and working herself into bad dreams.

"Enough," she muttered. She hopped off the bed, slapped the wrinkles out of her clothes, and started for the door. Then she paused. Would her parents let her out?

She decided to use the window instead. A breath of cool wind blew her silver-streaked blonde hair back as she lifted the window and screen. One deft maneuver had her out and scrambling down the trellis. She made no noise at all.

Twenty minutes later, she was jogging into the downtown plaza. The clusters of cars in the parking lot, the generic storefront signs, and the mobs of careless teenagers shrieking and laughing all made her feel normal again. Her shoulders relaxed and she slowed to a walk.

Ridiculous, she thought of her parents. *Insane. They've lost it. Or they're just messing with my head. Some technique they learned in a parenting magazine.*

She dimly wondered what lesson they were trying to teach her by making her so miserable, but a familiar voice broke her thoughts.

"Jenny!"

Eddie was strolling the sidewalk outside of the mall entrance. Next to him, to Jennifer's surprise, was Skip.

"Hey, Eddie. What're you up to?"

"Patrolling for hot chicks. Hey, we found one!" Eddie seemed embarrassed by his own lame joke. "Jenny, you meet Skip yet? He's new in town."

"Yeah." She nodded briefly at Skip. "We're in science with Ms. Graf together. Hey."

"Hey yourself, Jenny."

"It's *Jennifer*." It came out colder than she meant.

Skip smirked. "You sure are touchy, Jenny."

They stared at each other for a few seconds. Neither backed down.

"Aaanyway," Eddie interjected, "Skip and I are on a mission for ice cream before my dad comes to pick us up. You want to join us, Jenny . . . er . . . ifer?"

"If your ride's coming soon, we can go on without you," Skip added. There was a trace of defiance in his voice and eyes—almost as if he were daring Jennifer to blow off her ride.

"I walked. I've got all night." She took two steps forward, right into Skip's face. "I'd love to go with you, *Eddie*."

"We'd better move double-time," said Eddie with a glance at his watch.

The ice cream stand was at the other side of the mall. They walked outside, Eddie between Skip and Jennifer and talking the whole way. He seemed oblivious to the fact that both of his friends kept glaring at each other. After a few minutes, Jennifer found she preferred the sight of the bare, bright sliver of moon in the western sky.

They ordered quickly and then jogged back—gingerly holding their overfilled cones—to the mall entrance where Eddie's dad would meet them.

In fact Hank Blacktooth was already there in his dusty brown pickup truck, motor idling. Mr. Blacktooth was a glimpse of a future Eddie—if Eddie was fated to get heavier, hairier, and angrier. He glared at Eddie as the three kids approached the passenger door.

"You're late."

Eddie held up his watch. "You said six-thirty . . ."

"That was three minutes ago." Mr. Blacktooth held out his thick wrist. The stark digital watch read 18:33.

Eddie sighed. Skip looked at them both with a question on his face, but Jennifer knew Eddie's father better than to do anything but stare off in the distance.

"Can we give Jenny a ride home, too?"

"I've only got room in the cab for three. She'll have to ride in the back."

Jennifer opened her mouth to say she'd rather walk, but Eddie stopped her. "Geez, Dad, show a little chivalry. She doesn't have to do that. I'll hop in the back. She and Skip can ride up front."

Without another word, Eddie stepped aside and vaulted into the back of the truck.

Alarmed, Jennifer looked from Eddie to his father to Skip . . . and back to Eddie's father. Hank Blacktooth's eyes narrowed. In awkward silence, Skip and Jennifer sidled into the cab. Their seat belts made uncomfortable snaps, and then they were off.

It was an interminable minute before anyone spoke. "So, Skip. You were saying on the way here that your dad works in construction."

Skip was drying his palms on his jeans. Jennifer almost nudged him before the boy suddenly recognized the question and blurted out, "Yeah."

"Has he had much success lately?"

"Well, I don't follow it much, but Dad seems pretty happy, or as happy as he's been since Mom passed on. He was talking at dinner last night about finishing some municipal contract work he's been doing for years . . ."

They went on like this for a while. Hank Blacktooth was a real estate developer, and Skip calmed down and seemed to know enough about property and development to make small talk. Jennifer found her ambivalence about this odd boy shift into faint admiration at his increasing poise, squashed as he was between two strangers.

Of course, she knew Eddie's father would not ask *her* any questions. Ever since that day nearly seven years ago, when they had caught their son and the new girl next door playing an innocent game of "doctor" in the backyard, Mr. and Mrs. Blacktooth had treated Jennifer like a leper. They all but forbade contact between their families.

Eddie had managed to remain friendly over the years. But he never challenged his parents openly. Instead, he sought Jennifer out on school grounds, gave her quick pecks on the cheek when they sneaked a walk home together, and even dared an occasional visit to the Scales's house, where he always got a warm reception from Jennifer's mother.

"How's your mom, Jennifer?"

The icy tone startled Jennifer out of her reverie. Did he just ask her a question?

"Fine," she maneuvered. "She's working on a grant for the hospital."

"Yeah, she's still a nurse, isn't she?"

"Still a doctor, actually. Surgical chief."

Jennifer meant the correction kindly, but Blacktooth's quick look made her swallow.

"The folks at church still ask after her."

"After all these years?" Jennifer tried to sound breezy, but inside she was burning. Her mother had tried to become an active member of the local church when they first moved to Winoka, but some vicious gossip about her husband and another woman had driven her out within a year. Since the gossip had started soon after the Blacktooths freaked out over Jennifer, she heavily suspected them.

"She and your father still getting along all right?"

Jennifer just clenched her teeth. At first, it was in restraint. But suddenly, it was for an entirely different reason: terrible pain shot up her spine and through her jaw. *"Aaach!"*

Skip flinched. "Are you all right?"

Like that, the pain was gone. Jennifer rubbed the back of her neck. "I guess. Did we run over something?"

Mr. Blacktooth muttered irritably.

Another flare of pain swirled around her rib cage. Her hands flew up to her sides. *"Gaaagh!"*

Skip's eyes were wild. "Mr. Blacktooth, I think she's going to be sick!"

Until now, Jennifer had forgotten all about the conversation with her parents that afternoon. Meeting Eddie and Skip, getting cones, and running into Mr. Blacktooth had all seemed so normal for a while. But the reality of her situation came crashing down on her.

Her parents weren't crazy. They weren't using some weird parenting technique. She knew it, in her bones.

Literally.

Her teeth began to tingle and slide against each other. She coughed uncontrollably, and before she could slap her hand to her mouth, she spat blood on her palm.

"Mr. Blacktooth, I think we need to get her to a hospital!" There was no hiding the panic in Skip's voice.

The truck swerved to the curb and stopped short. Mr. Blacktooth muttered a curse, and then reached over Skip to shake Jennifer by the shoulder. "Coughing blood! What are you, on drugs? What did you just take?"

"She mainlined chocolate chip ice cream, not heroin!" screamed Skip. He waved his awkwardly long arms in the air. "What's the matter with you? Drive to the hospital!"

Jennifer didn't give them the chance. She reached down and unfastened the seat belt with her bloody hand while opening the door with the other. Then she scrambled out of the car and ran, through the yard and past the house into another yard, and out of sight.

Eddie called out to her from the back of his father's truck, but she could not hear her childhood friend. The blood was boiling in her ears.

The journey home was the most frightening experience of Jennifer's life. Alone, staggering through the dark, unable to hear beyond the confines of her crackling skull, Jennifer felt new sensations, most of it unbearable pain, in every corner of her body.

Not just her teeth, but her entire upper and lower jaws were flaring. Her shoulder blades felt like they were splitting open and piercing skin. Her spinal cord curled and stretched.

She screamed and then flinched. A roar of an animal

burst through the chaos in her ears. *A lion or an alligator?* There was no one around her, though some of the bushes nearby cast deep shadows.

Pine Street was quiet, with no joggers and only an occasional car. Most people were settling into prime-time television or a late dinner. Jennifer was both glad of this and alarmed—she didn't want anyone else to see what she knew was about to happen, but she didn't know if she could make it back home without help.

The veins under her skin thickened and rose. Blue tinted her hands, then her wrists, then her arms. Her hair cleaved itself to her neck and shoulders; she could feel strands pressing beneath skin and weaving among capillaries.

She let out another scream—the animal roared again—and stumbled to the sidewalk. Her knees scraped the ground, but she felt something tough under her jeans, something like leather, take the blow. An unbearable heat rose in her throat. It was hard to breathe.

"Mooooom! Daaaaad!" Her voice was slower and deeper.

Over her lengthening blue snout, Jennifer tried to spot home. It was less than a block away, but the lights were off. Where had her parents gone? They were likely out looking for her, probably frantic. She should have stayed in her room. They would know what to do. It would still be horrible, but at least they would be there.

She had no idea what would happen to her next, and the thought terrified her.

"Mooooom!" She coughed. What felt like vomit poured out of her mouth. A ball of flame singed her gums on the way out. The fire coursed over the paved sidewalk for a few feet.

Her eyes glazed over and she crumpled to the ground.

But she could still see, still feel, even hear? *Yes,* she could hear better now. A car coming, tires shrieking, a door opening, and then her mother's voice.

"Jennifer!"

Hands pulled at her legs. Trusting the touch of her parents, Jennifer let herself slip into unconsciousness.

She woke up to the familiar hum and vibration of the family minivan. Her parents had put down the backseat, and she was lying, curled up, in the cargo space.

The first thing Jennifer noticed about herself was that everything still ached.

The second thing was the astoundingly obvious horn perched at the tip of her snout, right before her eyes.

She turned to look at the rest of herself.

It was just as they had warned her. She saw the body of a large and mysterious lizard. Leathery, electric blue scales gave way to horizontal silver stripes, all the way into a slender forked tail. The belly of the lizard—*her* belly—was soft gray.

She was larger than she had been before, and a bit longer—much longer, if you counted the tail. Strange new muscles rippled with every movement she made. Five-inch claws tipped her powerful hind legs.

And she had *wings!* Two of them, folded neatly along her back. Jennifer moved her elbow, and one unfolded. She wiggled her fingers, and tiny batlike claws at the end of that wing waved back.

She fainted again.

* * *

The next time Jennifer woke up, she did not look back at her new lizard body. Instead, she stretched her neck until she could see past the middle row seat. Her mother was in the driver's seat. Beyond the windshield, the crescent moon was lifting higher into the nighttime sky.

She began to chew her tongue thoughtfully.

"Ouch!"

Of course. Sharper teeth. Jennifer chided herself for the near tongue piercing. Elizabeth turned briefly.

"You're awake?"

Even this first hint of normal conversation made Jennifer seethe with resentment. "What, can't you see my monster eyes glowing in the dark?"

Elizabeth turned around again. "Oh, yes. I can now. They're beautiful. Silver, darling. How do you feel?"

"I'm a dragon, Mother. I feel like a freak. No, beyond freak. Like a monster."

Her mother didn't reply right away. "You won't feel like a monster forever."

Jennifer hissed. It sounded very dangerous, which only made her angrier. "I feel that way now."

No response.

"Where are we going?"

"Grandpa Crawford's place."

That made sense. Her father's father had a quiet, secluded place out on the lake.

Plus, she liked Grandpa Crawford. Every Christmas, he came downstate with a truckful of presents, mostly books. He always skipped the ritual "how big you've grown" speech. Every summer, she'd visit his farm for a week. She loved relaxing in his enormous sitting room surrounded by crammed bookshelves, and she fondly remembered sitting on his lap as a small girl and hearing the most outrageous stories. Even now, she could picture his twinkling gray eyes . . .

"Oh." It came home to her. "Him, too?"

"Well, of course. After all, your father . . ."

"Where *is* Dad?"

Her mother nodded to the right side of the minivan. Jennifer looked out the window. Not twenty feet from their car, a dark and winged shadow soared. It kept pace easily with them along the edge of the highway.

The reptilian head turned toward them, and Jennifer saw the gray lining her father's silver eyes.

CHAPTER 4

The New Weredragon

Crawford Thomas Scales was a man who had made his fortune in unusual agriculture and ranching. His estate sprawled over hundreds of acres, most of it farmland and forested hills surrounding a generous lake. A crumbling stone wall stretched for miles around his property, more of a landmark than a real barrier to trespassers. But Grandpa Crawford didn't see many of those anyway, since no stranger dared take the first few steps onto his property without a proper escort.

A single break in the southern edge of the wall allowed for a long, winding gravel driveway. On either side of the driveway, and stretching along the inside of most of the wall, were clusters of strange-looking hives. These hives contained bees of extraordinary size and temper. They never flew beyond the confines of their owner's property—but they relentlessly attacked any stranger foolish enough to enter. Worse, they appeared impervi-

ous to weather, and remained active even through the
harsh Minnesota winters.

Beyond the hives was a strip, a dozen acres thick, of
wildflowers. No two blossoms were alike—Jennifer could
never figure out how her grandfather grew such diverse
and amazing wildflowers—but each stood as a tiny and
unique monument to nature. These were primarily for the
benefit of the bees, but Grandpa Crawford occasionally
brought some around the countryside to sell to local
flower shops.

After the flowers came grazing pastures, with horses
on one side of the road and sheep on the other. Jennifer
didn't enjoy riding horses but had to admit her grandfather picked, bred, and raised some amazing animals.
There were two or three that she particularly liked: black
Arabians with faint white markings on the hooves.

The sheep, on the other hand, were too numerous and
short-lived for her to bother with—hundreds of them, left
to roam largely free over the gently sloping hills.

A brief band of untended grassland lay between the
pastures and the modest forest that surrounded both the
lake and Grandpa Crawford's cabin. Bur oak, black wal-
nut, red maple, and Norway spruce trees clustered together at the edges, and then gave way to a small open
meadow to the north. Set at the back of this meadow, on
the edge of the broad lake beyond, stood the cabin.

They called it the "cabin," but it was much larger than
any ordinary cabin, with room for at least a dozen guests.
It was enormous. Grandpa Crawford had built the place
himself, forty years ago, with additions every ten years.
The first story of the cabin was lined with stone and covered nearly four acres, for every building was attached—

garage, toolshed, supply house, even the barn. The wooden upper-story of the living quarters had a smaller footprint, and was pushed northward toward the lake.

Jennifer stared out the window at these landmarks for some time before she realized she was seeing them in the dark, in color, with crystal clarity. *Night vision—like a monster.* Her surroundings were so familiar, yet so completely different when seen through these eyes.

Her mother turned the minivan off of the driveway and drove carefully around the east end of the cabin until they could see the north side. The entrance to the barn was already open, and they drove right in. Jennifer recalled the layout of the house, and how she always thought it odd that everything was attached to each other with big swinging doors. The far end of the barn would lead into a large mudroom, and then into the kitchen, and then into a massive sitting room. The sitting room faced north through double-wide sliding doors onto a patio, and a short-cropped lawn, and the lake beyond.

It made perfect sense now, she thought as her mother stopped the car and got out, that Grandpa Crawford would have such a large living area, with such an entry. She could tell already that normal-sized rooms, normal-sized doors, and normal-sized porches just weren't an option for the next few days.

Elizabeth lifted the minivan's back door and waited.

Jennifer stared back. "What?"

"You need to get out now, unless you want to spend the entire week in the back of the van."

"Right . . ." Jennifer looked warily at her legs. She had no idea how to do this. She measured her mother, up and down. "I don't suppose you could carry me again?"

"You're about a hundred pounds heavier than you were two hours ago," her mother estimated. "Not exactly portable. Thought about going on a diet?"

"What a perfect time for fat jokes, Mother. After all, I just turned fourteen and morphed into a gigantic iguana."

"Actually," Jonathan called out from the far end of the barn, where he was working a claw into a deep groove beneath the frame of the double doors, "more eagle than iguana. Like dinosaurs, we weredragons have more in common genetically with birds than with reptiles. Your mother's actually done some research into this. As you develop your more raptorlike capabilities, you'll see what I mean . . ."

"And my father's first words come in the form of a biology lecture." Jennifer groaned. "I can see that I may have changed, but you two are as clueless as ever." She tried to step majestically out of the back of the minivan with her right wing claw, but misjudged her weight placement and ended up tumbling tail over head onto a bed of hay. The horses in stables to either side snorted— derisively, she was sure.

Jonathan sighed as his claw caught the hidden lever he sought, and the doors into the cabin proper swung inward. The mudroom lights came on automatically, and Jennifer took a good look at her father for the first time.

The first things that caught her eye were the three thin horns that pierced the back of his head. They shone silver, like his eyes. Jennifer self-consciously reached back and felt her own skull—yep, she could feel three evenly spaced spikes back there as well.

But unlike his daughter, Jonathan Scales had no nose horn. And there were other differences.

While her blue was a sharp, electric shade, his was a deeper, almost purplish hue. Black stripes crossed over his back and wings, and his belly was a truer blue than his back. His wings were much larger in proportion to his body than hers were, and the arms at the leading edge of each wing were thinner. And while her tail had two prongs at the end, his tail had a slender, tapered point. Overall, his build was slighter than hers . . . and thinner, Jennifer noted with some self-contempt.

"Liz, why don't you go on in. It doesn't look like Dad's having any guests over this cycle. He may have left a message. I'll stay in the barn and help Jennifer with her new motor skills."

"Grandpa Crawford isn't here?" From her sprawled position on the ground, Jennifer was disappointed and curious. If Grandpa was also a weredragon, shouldn't he also be in dragon form now? If so, wasn't home the place to be? If not, when would he be back? And what was this about guests and cycles? She had been to this cabin many times, but had never seen any guests other than herself and her parents.

"He probably left for the lake. He may come back later. Get up if you can," said Jonathan Scales, ignoring his daughter's pout. He raised his wings, pushed gently off the doorway with a hind leg, and floated onto the hay next to her. Elizabeth went inside.

Jennifer squirmed on the ground. Flipped on her back like this, it wasn't easy to get up. She wriggled, got nowhere, and groaned. "This is so embarrassing."

"Fold your wings in and roll," he suggested.

She did, and was soon on all fours, her hind legs pushing her fat bottom higher up into the air than it ever had been in fourteen years, and her wing claws grasping at the ground fruitlessly. Her snout was in the dirt. All she could see was the hay two feet in front of her.

"The humiliation just never stops, does it?"

"Push off on your front claws a bit, so your head's off the ground . . . there you go . . ."

This was better. Now Jennifer was crouched like a cat ready to spring. She was certain she couldn't move, but she felt somewhat poised as long as she stood still.

"Walking is not a dragon's forte," Jonathan explained. "Even trampler dragons prefer galloping and leaping to a simple walk. But you'll have to learn a simple step or two before you can even think about flying."

He took her through the basics. Jennifer quickly learned that four-legged creatures have more independent movement of legs than bipeds like humans. She discovered she needed to keep her hind legs a half step ahead of the front ones, and she needed to use a scratch-and-pull method with her batlike wing claws to get anywhere. Progress was not easy. She was still pouting, and her father seemed determined to ignore her mood. So he talked more and more, and she said less and less, and before long the walking lesson was a nearly uninterrupted stream of words from the elder dragon.

"Bend your leg a bit more, that's it, keep your wings in closer to your body or you'll just zigzag. No, more, there, now scratch and pull, not bad at all for a first day! No, see, you fell because you weren't looking up. . . . Wow, that looked like it hurt. . . ."

"Okay, enough lessons!" she announced, after maybe ten minutes. "I can do enough to get inside and go to bed."

Her heart sank as she remembered her size. How would she fit through a bedroom door, much less in a bed?

Jonathan didn't seem worried about that. "Sure, okay. This is a lot to take in. But there *are* one or two things we should go over tomorrow—"

"Whatever," she groaned. She scratched and pulled her way across the barn, then delicately navigated the three wide wooden steps . . . and then nearly somersaulted through the open doors as she stepped on the tip of her wing with a hind leg. *"Aaargh!"*

Grandpa Crawford had left only two words for a message: CRESCENT VALLEY. The letters were scrawled with charcoal; a large piece of it was left on the floor of the sitting room, next to the newsprint he had written on. Neither parent would tell Jennifer what Crescent Valley was or when they expected her grandfather back—and they reminded her that sleep was probably a good idea.

The sitting room was, as Jennifer remembered it, quite spacious. The plush couches and chairs were already up against the walls, which were carved with oak shelves filled with leather-bound books. The sundry titles on these had always fascinated Jennifer. *The Withered Head*, *Hornets You Can Breed*, *Four-Dimensional Mapping*, and so on. Some of them, such as *Early Wyrms That Got the Bird* and *Shapes That Never Shift*, took on new meaning to her now.

Carefully retracting her claws so that she wouldn't scrape the hardwood floors or tear at the furniture, she edged up to one shelf of books that had always been her and Grandpa Crawford's favorite. She felt a tear in her silver, alien eye as she recalled the subject of the fantastic tales he told best—dragons.

Well, duh, she thought now.

There they all were—modern classics like *The Hobbit*, various tales of the Chinese dragon Nv Wa, and children's versions of more complex works like the story of Saint George the Dragon Slayer and *Beowulf*.

One book lay atop all the others—an oversized, flat leather volume with deeply worn edges. Jennifer reached out with a wing claw and grasped the binding. The title was in gold letters: *Grayheart's Anatomy*.

Jennifer did not say this as openly or often as she used to, but she admired her mother's work as a doctor. She knew that biology was her favorite of all the sciences, even though she had just started her own high school course in it. Working with living things, understanding what makes them move and breathe and see, was all utterly fascinating to her. And *Grayheart's Anatomy* represented the intersection of that interest and the love of dragons that Grandpa Crawford put into his stories.

It was the journal of an eighteenth-century explorer in North America who had come upon the body of a recently deceased dragon, taken it apart, and studied it. The layers of skin, the organs, the bone structure—all was in exquisite, illustrated detail. It used close study of the creature's anatomy to make guesses at how it lived, hunted, slept, fought, and even fell in love.

The pages were large and thick enough for Jennifer to flip through them, if she laid the book on the floor. She did so, while tears welled up. This wasn't a fanciful examination of a fictional corpse. This was *her*, or something very like her. Every muscle pulled back for analysis, every chamber of the upper and lower hearts split open for discovery . . .

Upper and lower hearts? The thought struck her cold. She put one claw over her left breast.

Thu-thump, thu-thump.

Then she let the claw slide slowly down and to her right side, about where her appendix would be if she were a human girl.

Da-da-thump, da-da-thump.

After all the pain of the metamorphosis, seeing her new body for the first time, observing her father, trying to walk, and everything else, this finally brought home the full impact of what had happened to her.

"All right, to hell with sleep," she told her parents, who were rolling out large oriental rugs at the other end of the room. "I have questions, and I want answers."

They stopped short, dragon and woman, then blinked and nodded in unison.

"First question. Why did you wait until *today* to tell me this? It isn't fair! I've had no time—"

"You're right, Jennifer. It isn't fair. We're sorry."

She was stunned at how quickly her father apologized.

"But we didn't know this was going to happen so quickly. We thought we had years. Most weredragons don't experience their first change until later—sixteen or seventeen years old, at the youngest. Then we saw how fast and strong you were getting, but we still thought it was all a few months away. The dragonflies at school were a complete shock—as you'll learn, that sort of thing is a practiced skill among elder dragons.

"As soon as you did it, we knew we had to tell you so you would be prepared. So we did. But even earlier today, we didn't know for sure if you would turn this lunar cycle, or next, or even a year from now."

"So what am I doing like this, two years early?"

"We're not sure." Jonathan sighed. "It's probably because your mother isn't a weredragon. You're a hybrid. That would probably affect you."

Jennifer cringed. "So let me get this straight. Not only am a I freak among *people*, I'm a freak among *dragons*, as well?"

"Honestly, Jonathan," her mother hissed. "A *hybrid*? The *dog* is a hybrid. Could you come up with less insulting language?" She turned to Jennifer desperately. "Please don't see yourself that way. I know this is hard, but . . ."

"SHUT UP, MOTHER, YOU *DON'T* KNOW. YOU CANNOT POSSIBLY SEE THIS THROUGH MY EYES."

The three of them stood silently for a while. Then Jennifer asked her next question.

"Dad, we look pretty different from each other. Is this *also* because I'm a freak?"

He paused and scratched behind his middle horn, clearly dreading the answer. "You appear to have some unusual characteristics."

"I'll take that as a yes. Next question: Who's taking care of Phoebe?"

"I called the Blacktooths with the cell phone, on the way up," her mother said quietly. "Eddie will go over and feed the dog until we get back."

"Am I going to be like this for a few days?"

"Four or five."

"Then I'd like Phoebe to be up here with me."

"Sweetheart, the dog—"

"I'd like her up here with me." Jennifer crouched down and curled into a ball. She would have thought even her parents could understand this.

"Okay," Elizabeth agreed. "I'll go to get her tomorrow morning."

"Fine." Jennifer stretched her neck out. "Do the Blacktooths—does Eddie—know about weredragons?"

"No," her father answered quickly. "As you can imagine, Jennifer, many people would get upset if they learned the truth. And we have some enemies you will learn about

later. There are not many of our kind left. Those who survived Eveningstar have been hiding since. You'll meet
them once you're ready."

"Eveningstar." Memories came back to Jennifer of the
early morning of her fifth birthday. "That was our home.
Someone attacked the town."

"Yes."

"You woke me up, and we escaped . . ."

"Yes."

". . . over the river in a boat . . ."

"Yes. Well, no. You and your mother were actually riding on my back as I swam. You seemed nervous, since
you had never seen me as a dragon before. So I used my
voice to convince you who I was. That worked well
enough to get you on my back and over the river."

Jennifer closed her eyes. "There were fires all over the
town. We saw them from the other side of the river. And
there was screaming—I don't remember what."

"It was a war, Jennifer." Her mother was talking now.
"The weredragons were very nearly exterminated. Families and friends who had grown up together for generations scattered. We each moved to different towns,
hoping to hide. There's no one else in Winoka who knows
the truth about you and your father."

"That's not completely true, is it?" asked Jennifer. She
was trying to be calm, but as she pieced more things together, she became angry—at her parents, at herself, and
at her neighbors. "The rumors that went around town
when we first moved. The way they made you miserable
at church. They must have known something."

"They did probably feel that something was not quite
right with us," Jonathan said carefully. "It's impossible
to keep a secret like this completely. Crescent moons

happen at very inconvenient times, and the stories we told to cover the truth may have changed as they passed from person to person. Your mother and I felt there may have been a presence there at the church that was not completely friendly to us. Rumors found fertile ground, and I was not around often enough to help your mother dispute them."

Jennifer saw her mother's hand squeeze his wing claw as he said this. She decided to change the subject.

"When will I meet some other weredragons? I mean, besides you and Grandpa."

"Soon," her father said. "While we've been careful to keep you away from this farm during crescent moons, you'll find it's a very different place around then. This is a refuge, one of only a few left, where we can stay away from prying, unfriendly eyes."

"And I'll change like this, every crescent moon, for five days, just like you?"

"Pretty much. There are small differences from one weredragon to the next. During the waxing of the moon leading to the first quarter, and the waning of the moon into a new moon, our bodies feel intense pressure to change. You'll need a minimum of four days in this state, but most weredragons need five. But for however long, it happens on both crescents, every time."

Jennifer slapped her wing to her forehead as another thought struck. "This is going to keep happening, twice a month! I'm going to miss school! My friends are going to figure this out—Eddie may not know about us now, but what he and Skip saw last night—"

"They saw nothing," said Elizabeth. "When I talked to Mr. Blacktooth on the phone, he was quite positive you were on drugs. Of course, I assured him that you were not. The story we will use with people like the Black-tooths, and school, and everyone else is that you are falling seriously ill. Something chronic, and perhaps even incurable."

"Lovely. You know, I can already hear and feel the air whistling as my friends abandon me."

"Give your friends some credit, Jennifer. They're not that shallow. They'll understand your absence and support you when you're there. We'll keep the name of your 'clinic' to ourselves to avoid visitation requests, and set up a long-term plan before the end of the school year."

" 'Long-term'? You mean we might have to move?"

"Yes, probably. I'm sorry, ace, but a school-age were-dragon presents tons of opportunity for you to be discovered, or worse, hurt and killed."

Jennifer's face fell. "I'll never go back to high school. Never go to a prom, or play varsity soccer."

Elizabeth took a step forward. "You'll miss those experiences. But you'll do and see things that no one else will. Things *I* never will. You said it yourself—I'll never see the world through your eyes. No one can."

"That's not exactly what I meant—"

"You know that we still love you, more than anything else in the whole world. Right?" Her mother seemed honestly unsure of her daughter's answer.

"Hmmph." Jennifer felt herself start to soften a bit, but would not allow it. She looked away.

"Do you have any other questions?" Jonathan asked.

"Thousands. But that's enough for tonight," she said grudgingly. "You guys are right, I should get some sleep."

Elizabeth pulled a couple more oriental rugs out of the closet. She unrolled these across the hardwood floor of the sitting room while her husband shut the patio doors.

"We're all sleeping here, in this room? But there are plenty of guest rooms, and the beds are large enough!"

"It wouldn't be right to leave you alone, on your first night," Jonathan answered. "Besides, your grandpa hates it when your mother and I use his bed."

Elizabeth couldn't totally stifle her giggle.

"Aw, yuck," Jennifer groaned. The image of her parents smooching in bed together was particularly disturbing, if not downright revolting, given the shapes she saw before her now.

"Relax," said Jonathan. "What you're thinking is downright impossible. Anything that would gross you out happens *outside* of a crescent moon—"

"*Please* stop talking, Dad."

Elizabeth flicked off the lights, and only the barest slice of moonlight ventured through the patio doors. It was enough so Jennifer could see her father curl up against the sofa, and her mother lie down next to him and set her head against his belly.

She stayed in her own corner of the sitting room, spread out on top of a green and brown runner they had just unrolled. *This is cute,* she sniffed to herself. *Just like on the wildlife channel, except with oriental rug accents.*

CHAPTER 5

Sheep, Bees, and Fish

This time, Jennifer knew it was a dream right away.

First, she was flying, which of course only happened in dreams. Second, there were hundreds of oranges and soccer balls in the air, falling like hailstones. She knew she had to kick them all back up into the sky, though she didn't have the faintest idea why.

She slid through the air, spreading human hands and feet to dart toward one target—an orange. *Fwap,* the kick sent it up and back through the clouds. Next was a soccer ball. *Fwap.* Another and another—*fwap-fwap.*

Then the oranges and soccer balls turned black. Jennifer squinted to get a better look. They weren't oranges or balls anymore. Thick, bloated bodies with spindly legs cascaded down from the thunderheads.

It was raining spiders.

Several dropped with shrill cries onto her head. She

felt their hairy appendages squeeze her skull as their fangs danced right before her eyes . . .

"All right!" shouted Jennifer to no one in particular as she started awake and slapped at the empty air around her nose horn. "Enough with the dreams already!"

She was alone in the sitting room, and the faint mid-morning sun filtered through the patio doors. They were open enough for her to smell the chill of autumn.

Under daylight, she could see the colors of the forest and lake outside more clearly than she had last night. Grandpa Crawford's trees were gorgeous this time of year, every color a leaf could ever turn now on display—purple, gold, orange, brown, yellow, and stubborn green. A few less brilliant hues continued around the large lake. The lake itself was calm, with sparse waves cresting and disappearing quickly over clear water.

The house was silent. Curious, she ambled on all fours through the rooms until she came to the barn.

The minivan was gone.

With a brief gulp of panic, Jennifer clawed her way quickly across the barn. She pushed the large doors open and peered outside. No one was there.

"Mom? Dad?" She tried not to sound alarmed as she scurried awkwardly around the northeast corner and scrambled up onto the patio. There was a reason why they had left, she told herself. Only Mom could drive the car, so she must have run an errand.

Then she thought of last night. Of course, she had gone to get Phoebe. Jennifer had demanded it. She would be back soon with the dog.

That left her father . . .

"Heads up!"

Jennifer looked up just in time to duck away from the huge, furry ball leveled like a bomb at her skull. She briefly thought of the giant spiders from her dream, but when the missile landed she calmed down, if only a little.

It was a sheep, one of Grandpa Crawford's. Its matted wool was streaked with blood, and its hind legs were broken. It was bleating in terror.

"Dad!" This didn't strike Jennifer as funny at all.

He landed on the porch next to the sheep and balanced a hind claw on the sheep's throat. "Sorry, I didn't see you come out until I had let go of it."

"What are you doing mauling sheep anyway?" She was pretty sure she could guess the answer and she began to feel sick. "Grandpa's going to get really mad at you."

"I think you know as well as I do that he won't. Why do you think he goes through more sheep than he can breed every year? He can't live on honey alone, and he likes his horses too much to eat them."

Jennifer was relieved she wouldn't have to watch her father eat an Arabian stallion. Then she was disgusted all over again. "Ugh. That's not just for you, is it?"

"Of course not. I've already eaten. I brought this one back so I could show you how to skin and cook them. After that, we'll see to the horses, and then I'll give you your first flying lesson."

The word "cook" settled Jennifer's stomach a bit. The word "flying" pricked her imagination.

Then Jonathan Scales twisted the hind claw that clenched the sheep's throat, and the crack and gurgle that followed had her sick to her stomach again. "Aw, *Dad* . . ."

"It's a sheep, ace, not a kindergartner. You eat this sort of thing all the time."

That brought another question to Jennifer's mind. "Um, Dad, we don't ever eat . . . *people* . . . do we?"

Jonathan looked at his daughter with silver-eyed patience. "No matter how much you try to tell yourself otherwise, Jennifer, you are not a monster. You are not a freak. You still eat the same things you did before yesterday, and you'll still like doing the things you did before yesterday. We're going to cook and eat our meals in as civilized a way as we can manage. We'll have trout tonight for dinner, just like we always do here at Grandpa's. I'll make risotto to go with it—your triple-chambered stomach will find your mother's cooking as horrific as your single-chambered stomach did."

She choked back a giggle.

"You can use the same charcoal and paper Grandpa has lying around to do sketches. Your wing claw can manage it. There's even a soccer ball in the garage, once you get your balance back. You are still Jennifer Scales, and you're all the things that make you a terrific daughter.

"I'm not saying there won't be new things to learn. But if you see them as additions, and not subtractions, you'll have an easier time with this. Understand?"

Jennifer nodded slowly.

"Great. Now let's gut this sheep and roast it!"

It wasn't as gruesome as she thought it would be. Her father showed her how to use her claws to skin the animal, slice open the belly, separate the edibles from the nonedibles, and slice the meat into manageable chunks. She had an uncle on her mother's side who used to treat venison for hunters, so she had seen this sort of thing before. It wasn't completely enjoyable, but it seemed more like butcher's work than a beast's.

With ten neat cuts of meat lying on the porch, she looked up at her father with something approaching pride.

"Excellent. Now we cook 'em."

Grandpa Crawford had an enormous grill on one end of the porch—it was three times the size of most grills. Jonathan poked a wing claw under the grate, arranged the coals beneath, and then shot a bullet of flame out of his nostrils. The coals began burning immediately.

"All right. Put those cuts on there, and put the cover down. From here on in, it's just like barbecue."

"Neat." Jennifer couldn't hide a smile. "I don't suppose there's any ketchup in the fridge?"

As Jennifer finished—surprising herself by downing all ten pieces in ten ketchup-tinted gulps—the minivan drove up onto the north lawn. A familiar shape was poised in the passenger seat with its head out of the window.

"Phoebe!"

She wasn't sure how the collie-shepherd would react to a seven-foot-long reptile with a family member's voice, but to Jennifer's unending delight, there was never a question in the dog's mind. Phoebe leapt out of the open window and raced up the porch steps to lick her pack sister's scaly face. Then, in a black dash, she was off around the house and through the forest.

Jonathan grinned. "Off to find sheep of her own. She never could resist herding them."

"How's it going?" called out Elizabeth. She was getting something out of the car.

"We've had breakfast. I'd like to do a few more things, maybe get in a bit of flying before lunch."

"Well, I got what you asked. You sure this is safe?"

Of all the things her mother could have pulled out of the minivan, Jennifer never imagined she would see a trampoline. She looked at her father with startled eyes.

"It's safe," he assured both of them. "But before we get to that, we need to cover fire-breathing. Could you check on the horses for me, Liz?" He turned to Jennifer. "I started the fire that cooked your breakfast, but you'll need to learn how to do your own fire-breathing if you want to have anything but raw meat for yourself."

"Okay," Jennifer agreed. With a full stomach, a good night's sleep, and a growing acceptance that her transformation wasn't immediately fatal, she was ready to learn a few things. Plus, the thought of her crawling on her belly and eating uncooked food for five-day stretches did not sit well.

Elizabeth set the trampoline against the porch, and then went off to check on the horses, Phoebe, and the sheep.

"Come on." Her father gestured. "Let's practice into the lake, with the wind at our backs."

Fire-breathing, as it turned out, involved just about every vocal action short of actually speaking. A cough, a snort, a growl, even a sneeze—each of these, her father explained, opened a small valve at the back of the throat that released the fire element. Then, as with speech, the placement of the lips, tongue, and teeth did the rest.

While sneezes generated short but impressive fireworks from the nostrils, a rough clearing of the throat issued a volcanic flow that cascaded over the grass and into the lake. Most spectacular of all, a shrill whistle let loose a volley of flame rings that grew as large as hula hoops.

"Check this out," he told her, calling Phoebe at the top of his lungs. "Once in a while, like when you're off at summer camp, your mother and I bring the dog up here during crescent moons and teach her tricks."

Phoebe came racing like a dark dart around the opposite end of the house from where she had disappeared. The moment she saw Jonathan rear up on his hind legs, she stopped about twenty yards away and crouched low in anticipation.

"Phoebe—*circus!*"

The dog stood up. Jonathan let out a short whistle, and a ring of fire ripped out of his mouth. With no steps at all, the dog leapt through the blazing hoop as it roared over her position, did a half-twist in the air, and then landed brilliantly on all fours.

Jennifer burst out laughing. Phoebe raced to a point about twenty yards from her and crouched down as before, obviously expecting Jennifer to do the same.

The three of them played like this for a while. The longer the whistle, the greater the number of hoops Phoebe had to jump through. She could manage up to three, but singed her tail if asked to do more than that.

After an hour or so, Jennifer felt in good enough spirits that she nodded when her father suggested they begin flying lessons.

"This isn't going to be like fire-breathing," he warned her. "That comes as naturally to a dragon as, well, breathing. But flying won't come any easier than walking did when you were a toddler. You fell down. A lot. Now you'll be higher up."

"Great." Jennifer sighed.

"Don't worry too much. A dragon's bones and sinews are incredibly resilient. You won't break or twist a thing. Just your ego, once or twice. Plus, we have this!"

He grabbed a bar of the trampoline with a hind claw

and shoved off the ground with the other. "Meet me out by the wildflower fields. Trees and water make for a poor first flight." Weaving his way through the elms and pines, he disappeared.

Jennifer trudged her way on all four claws back down the gravel driveway. It was at least a half mile to the wildflower fields. By the time she got there, her throat was dusty and her belly sore from all the scratching and pulling. She was more than ready to learn how to get her carcass off the ground.

Jonathan was bouncing on the trampoline, humming a jaunty tune with smoke smoldering from his nostrils. "A beautiful day to spend out in the sunshine!" he called out. "And a good day to get up in the air, too. Come over here, ace. I'll give you a hand up . . ."

He stepped off as she sought her balance in the rubbery center. If walking on four legs was difficult, navigating a bouncy, slippery material was even worse. Up and down Jennifer jarred, a jumble of wings and horns. It was impossible to stop. She decided to wait out the embarrassment on her butt, lolling up and down miserably. Her previous enthusiasm drained away.

"Perk up, camper! You're learning something amazing."

"What, hopping on my ass?"

Her father snorted with laughter, letting a cloud of steam out from between his teeth. Jennifer almost smiled back, though a part of her was determined to stay grumpy. "All right, what do I do?"

"We'll start off with simple bouncing, straight up and down. Just like everyone does. Sitting down is fine, the idea is to get the feel for liftoff."

This was easy enough, since the trampoline hadn't really stopped jouncing her yet. She pushed off a bit harder to get up in the air, and before long she established a slow, steady rhythm.

"Good. Now, spread your wings on each up, and fold them on each down . . ."

This was harder, because her wings caught the south wind when unfolded, which moved her slightly out of position each trip into the air. Jennifer found herself adjusting her wings each time, to try and catch the wind different ways.

"Great! You're figuring out how the wind and your wings interact. There are four forces at work—gravity, lift, thrust, and drag. Your wings represent an incredible evolutionary leap that minimizes drag while allowing . . ."

"Dad."

"Yes?"

"If you want to minimize drag, you could talk less."

Jennifer let her hind legs down so that she was standing and jumping each time. Wings out, wings in, wings out, wings in . . . Suddenly, Jennifer kicked hard off the trampoline and waved her wings frantically. On the third beat, her wings caught wind, and she sailed at least thirty feet into the air.

"Nice!" she heard her father call. "Oh, keep flapping, or you'll come back down too fast."

She got the message right away as her bulk began to drop. Beating her wings again, she found another gust of air to support her weight, and she tilted her wings to take advantage of it. Now she was more than fifty feet up off the ground. The air was cooler up here. With wild eyes she took in the entirety of Grandpa Crawford's farm. There were the hives to the south, and the wall beyond, and if she turned a bit she could see the sheep scattering at the sight of her silhouette in the sky, and beyond them the trees, and the house, and the lake . . .

"KEEP FLAPPING OR YOU'LL LOSE LIFT!" Her father's voice right next to her startled her, and she flinched into an awkward shape. She immediately dropped ten feet.

"Cripes, Dad!" She regained composure and glared up at his hovering form. Unsolicited lectures on the ground were merely boring. At this altitude, they were dangerous!

After a few minutes of flapping, she began to get the hang of gaining and losing altitude. Her wings were getting tired, though, and she looked down at the ground with both longing and fear.

He seemed to read her mind. "As any pilot will tell you," he called out, "landing is easy. Landing *well* is hard. Aim for the trampoline again, and try to lose altitude a few feet at a time."

As she began her descent, she found relaxing and re-stretching her wings even harder than flapping them continually. It was like dropping bit by bit in a shaky helicopter, and her stomach turned once or twice after particularly steep pitches.

Looking down, she could see the trampoline far below, almost between her hind claws. She adjusted a bit to the left and headed for the center.

The heavy whistling in the trees to the north should have warned her what was coming, but neither Jennifer nor her father noticed the sudden crosswind until too late. She felt it like a shove in the back. In a split second she lost her shape and balance, and found herself diving feet first at a sharp angle to the ground. The wildflowers rushed up to greet her.

"Tilt your wings!" she heard her father cry.

She leaned forward in a panic and drew even with the ground, belly skimming the tips of the taller sunflowers and reedy grasses. It was like her first experience with a bicycle as a child—she was moving fast, her muscles were frozen, and she had no idea how to stop.

She passed out of the wildflower fields and into the bee fields, closer and closer to the ground. Dropping a leg to try to slow herself down was unthinkable; Jennifer had visions of tripping at thirty miles per hour and breaking her neck in the subsequent tumble. The best she could hope for was a glider landing on her belly. The grass looked soft . . .

A short hillock was all it took for Jennifer's right wing to catch the earth. The impact jarred her entire body, throwing her out of symmetry and sending her into exactly the kind of rolling tumble she had been trying to avoid—only this time, she was sent askew by the hit to her right side. Jennifer lost herself in a furious swirl of earth and sky.

At last, she crashed into something that felt like rotted wood. Her head spun and buzzed, and a sickly sweet smell filled her nostrils.

"Are you okay, Jennifer?" She heard her father's voice above her.

"Yeah . . ."

"Good. Now get out of there!"

A slow liquid oozed onto her belly. Thinking it was blood, she lifted her head up . . . and saw honey. Then she realized the buzzing wasn't in her head at all.

"Ah, sugar . . ."

"Out! Out!" her father called. She could have sworn he was chuckling. Hundreds of black dots converged on her position. With another curse, she kicked her way out of the pile of broken honeycomb that her landing had destroyed. Of course, she had no way to run. It was crawl or fly, and Jennifer didn't even stop to think. She just unfolded her wings, took two or three panicked steps with her hind legs, and then pushed herself up.

Miraculously—or so it seemed to her—it worked. Ten feet up, then twenty, then she was over the wildflowers again, leaving the angry swarm of bees far behind.

"Nice takeoff!" her father beamed as he swooped into position next to her. "I shouldn't have bothered with the trampoline. All we had to do is plop you on top of a beehive, and you perfected your technique just fine."

"Hilarious, Dad. How the heck do I get down?"

"Let's try a bit farther north, by the sheep pastures. They don't sting as hard."

"This isn't funny . . ."

"You didn't see it from my angle."

"I could have maimed myself!"

"Don't be ridiculous. Like I said, it will take more than a beginner's crash to hurt you. And no bug *you've* ever seen has a stinger long enough to pierce your hide. You could wear those bees as a winter coat. Now come on, we've got a landing to finish."

She followed him to the sheep pastures, but the words "no bug you've ever seen" stuck in her mind. Her mind went back to the butterfly in Ms. Graf's classroom, and the menacing cloud of dragonflies.

What bug might she see someday that she *did* have to worry about?

For the rest of the day, they worked on flying and landing. The only interruption was lunch. Elizabeth produced two vatfuls of slightly overcooked macaroni and cheese, and then stayed with them for the afternoon to watch her daughter's progress.

By the time the sun was low in the sky, Jennifer felt mildly comfortable taking off and landing in an open field. She ventured as high as a hundred feet once, but lost her nerve as she realized she was coasting over prickly pine trees. Two unusually large golden eagles swooped by her ear and convinced her to seek firm ground. It was enough—she decided as she landed without stumbling for the first time to applause from her mother and praise from her father—to get this far.

"Excellent!" her father cheered. "You've got a real gift for this, ace. Your grandfather had to work with me for at least three days. He finally lost his patience, took me up to the roof of the cabin, and shoved me off toward the lake. Speaking of which—"

He spread his wings and kicked off the ground, soaring into the air. Jennifer noticed his perfect, effortless form with a small twinge of jealousy. She struggled to follow him up, while her mother began a jog back to the cabin.

"I need to catch dinner," Jonathan explained. "You should just watch for this part, I think. No sense in you drowning just yet."

They turned north and let their wings stretch as they coasted over the lake. Jennifer tried not to think about the fact that landing here would be impossible, and that the tree-lined shore was hardly better terrain. Instead, she focused on following her father as he climbed in broad circles. Eighty, ninety, a hundred feet—Jennifer caught a small crosswind but shifted her wings quickly to compensate—two hundred feet, three hundred, and still Jonathan climbed.

Jennifer kept her head up. She knew the distant view of water and trees below would terrify her. They were going far higher than she ever had outside of an airplane.

When they reached five hundred feet, her father turned his head. "The first thing you have to do is follow the shadows. Clear your mind and keep your eyes on the water."

He looked down, and Jennifer reluctantly did the same. The setting sun cast an uneven light over the surface of the lake, and at first she couldn't make much out. But by letting her eyes relax, she found that she could both ignore the altitude and see small shapes underwater.

"You hover and wait until they come near the surface," she heard her father continue. "Then you dive. Okay, remember, just watch for now."

An instant later, her father plunged with his feet forward and down and wings stretched back behind him. He looked to Jennifer like a massive, indigo hawk.

Seconds later, just before he dove into the lake itself, he broke his own fall with a furious beating of wings, jabbed into the water with both hind legs, and plucked out two silvery shapes. He lifted off again, circled over the lake to the shore, and dropped the fish into a large plastic crate his wife had pulled out into the yard. Then he circled up to meet Jennifer again.

"Dad, I'll never be able to do that. That was crazy!"

"You'll be doing it by the end of the week. Tomorrow, if we have time."

Without waiting for an argument, he dove again, this time face first and with wings held close around his trunk and tail. Jennifer almost screamed when she saw his head slam right into the water, followed by his body with a surprisingly small splash. She hovered uneasily. Was that his shadow she saw? Yes, of course: it let out a stream of bubbles as it sliced through the water. He was much faster underwater than she would have expected.

A few seconds later, he emerged from the lake, this time with a larger shimmering shape in his mouth. Jennifer knew her fish well; she could tell even from this far that it was a walleye. It followed the trout into the plastic bin.

"I'll need to get about a dozen more like that," he panted upon rejoining her. "Should take only a few minutes. But you might want to get a bit lower, if that'll make you more comfortable. I'll go as fast as I can."

And he was off again. As he fished, the pair of eagles Jennifer had seen before flew a tight circle on the opposite end of the lake, occasionally sparing a sharp glance at this larger predator. She watched her father with something approaching regret—he was doing all the work, while she just tagged along. She had never liked that feeling, not even as a small child. They had always fished together when they came to Grandpa Crawford's lake. She would have her own pole, tackle, and bait; Grandpa even kept a special tackle box for her in his garage. Catching her own fish always felt special, and she hadn't needed help tying her line or setting the hook for years.

This, on the other hand, felt too much like her father wrapping his arms around her to guide the fishing pole, while one hand stayed on hers over the reel to make sure she didn't reel too fast or too slow. It chafed her.

Doesn't look that *hard,* she convinced herself as her father came up with his sixth and seventh fish. *And if I do it wrong, what happens? I get a little wet. Big deal.*

Jennifer fixed her eyes on the lake's surface, a bit away from where her father had just disturbed the water. Before long, she found them: three slender shadows, wriggling just under the surface of the lake. She let her feet down, pulled her wings up . . .

. . . and began to scream.

Like most insane water rides, the dive was more terrifying in the experience than the watching. At first, Jennifer was certain she was doing something wrong. Then a voice in the back of her mind spoke up.

Keep your head down. Eyes on the fish.

She saw the three shapes scatter at the sense of her shadow above them—drat, she had come in on them from the west, like an idiot. No stopping now. While two of the shapes bolted in opposite directions, one just shot straight ahead. She chose that one, and tilted her wings so that her diving path became less steep.

Claws out . . .

She saw her hind claws flex as they reached out in front of her. Her approach to the surface was perfect, the fish was right below her, she tilted back, back . . .

Wings! Flap wings, dork! Slow down! You overshot!

She lost sight of the fish as it disappeared below her nearly prone body. A desperate flap of wings broke her form, and she struggled to avoid plunging into the water. It worked, sort of—she slowed a bit, the fish tried to scoot past, and she flicked her hind leg into the water without thinking. Her claws pierced slime and scales, and she felt a brief thrill of victory.

Unfortunately, she was still moving, and she realized she had no idea how to pull up. On her back, with wings spread out like enormous air brakes, Jennifer did the only thing she could think of—she turned her wings forward to start flapping.

Had she been faster, or even a few feet above the water, this might have worked. But instead, the new shape sent her into a roll, and she skidded across the surface of the lake like a skipping stone. A few splashes ended with one large *sploosh,* and then she was floating on the surface on her back, a bit dazed . . .

. . . and with the fish still squirming, impaled on the back toe of her hind claw.

She raised her head and found her father, who was cruising toward her. "I GOT THE FISH!" she hollered. "I GOT THE FISH!"

With a vigorous flop, the fish loosened itself from her claw and dropped into the water with a light splash.

"Aaaaargh!" She immediately folded her wings up against her body, rolled over in the water, and dove.

Get back here, you slimy, stupid, hole-in-your-gut, useless excuse for a fish! It was hard for Jennifer not to take the rascal's escape personally. Two seconds ago, she had looked like a fool who had managed to catch a fish. Now, unless she caught that fish again, she just looked like a fool.

There it was—a wavering, glimmering shape ahead, trickles of blood escaping the puncture wound from both sides. She knew it would be easy enough to pluck off the surface when it died shortly, but that wasn't the point.

She heard a massive splash nearby, and saw her father's shape enter the water. *Oh, no, you don't, Dad. No help on this one. This fish is* mine!

With that last thought, she let out a furious hiss. To her great surprise, a cascade of flame escaped from her jaws and surged toward her prey, boiling the water as it passed. The tempest coursed over the fish and Jennifer lost sight of it for an instant.

Then, after the flames died and the water cooled, she saw the fish gently float to the surface, quite dead.

She followed it up. When her head broke into the chill autumn air, she heard something large thrashing in the water close by . . . and *laughing*?

The dead fish floated gently by her nose horn. It was charred, punctured, and half of it was missing. It was pathetic. It was beautiful.

Later that evening, with her father still chuckling, her mother giggling, risotto simmering, and the rest of the fish roasting, Jennifer still believed that her catch looked the best of the lot of them.

CHAPTER 6

Regression

The next few days passed agreeably enough. Jennifer continued to work on her flying and hunting, and found time for the occasional game of circus with Phoebe. During the evenings, she would try sketching with the large chunk of charcoal and newsprint that Grandpa Crawford used. It seemed a lost cause at first, but she eventually got the hang of moving her wing claw back and forth as fluidly as she would move a human hand, so that the charcoal made gentle, accurate strokes. Before long, she was sketching trees, water, and other shapes.

Despite her father's encouragement, however, she did not get the soccer ball out. Even with her successes this week, looking at the ball made it too easy to think about her friends, and how they would react if they ever found out how different and dangerous she was.

What would Eddie say? What would his parents say? And Susan? What would happen to her, and her family, if the town found out? Would they have to move? Would the truth follow them? Would she ever get to feel, or even act, normal again?

So the soccer ball stayed in the garage, and Jennifer stayed out of the garage.

The dreams, she was glad to see, settled down a bit. In fact, sleeping in her favorite vacation house, in her room, and even the (admittedly reassuring) presence of her parents was all almost pleasant.

The fourth morning at the cabin, she lay sprawled out on the grass, shooting smoke rings softly around Phoebe's long muzzle while the dog licked her nose horn. The cries of the nearby family of golden eagles punctuated the still air. Elizabeth was finishing some cold cereal on the porch, and her father had flown off somewhere before Jennifer had even woken up.

"Flying today should be good," she told her mother. They hadn't talked much all week; Jennifer figured they both had been trying to stay out of each other's way.

Elizabeth didn't answer right away. Jennifer lifted her head. "Mom?"

"I heard you. But I'm not sure your father will want you to fly today."

Jennifer raised her snout into the air. Her Dad had taught her how to tell if the weather was changing. "Temperature's crisp, not too bad. I don't smell much change on the wind. Am I wrong?"

Elizabeth gave a genuine smile. "I wouldn't know, dear. But whatever the weather, I think your father wants you to take it easy today. It is, after all, day five."

Day five. The words hit Jennifer like bricks. The crescent moon was ending. Of course it wouldn't do to be soaring through the air at two hundred feet if her body picked that time to change back into human form!

She wondered how much it would hurt. Getting larger and scalier had definitely not tickled. Would shrinking and growing hair feel any better? It seemed it might be less traumatic, but she couldn't be sure and didn't know if her father would give her an honest answer.

"So what're we going to do today? And where's Dad?"

"No plans, just do what you like. On the ground, that is. Your dad went to see your grandfather."

"Where *has* Grandpa been all this time, anyway? The note he left said 'Crescent Valley' but we never saw him around."

Her mother paused again.

"Never mind! I can tell I won't get a straight answer."

Elizabeth downed the milk left in her bowl in a single gulp. "You always were a perceptive girl."

Jonathan did not return until midday. Jennifer was sketching fish in the sitting room when her mother called her to the patio door and pointed. Two large shapes were pelting the surface of the lake with their wings.

They looked nearly identical—the colors on their backs and bellies, the three horns at the backs of their skulls, and even their toothy smiles. Jennifer supposed her grandfather was the slightly smaller one, since her father was taller than her grandfather as a human.

She examined the electric blue and silver skin across her wings, back, and double-pronged tail. Her nose horn and wider bulk had already made her feel different from her father, but now she saw just how different she was.

With a glare at her gene-pool-wrecking mother, Jennifer went out on the porch and watched her father and Grandpa Crawford reach the shore. Phoebe had been trying to herd some dry leaves blowing in the wind, but broke off and sped toward the dragons as they landed.

"Hey, Phoebe!" Grandpa Crawford's voice was tighter and higher than her father's, but it had the same congenial tilt to it. "Get the worm! Get the worm!" The smaller dragon held one wing up and wriggled one talon of the wing claw a few feet above the dog's head. Phoebe obliged, jumping up and poking the talon with her nose. Then she bolted away from Grandpa Crawford and up the porch steps, where she tried to share her enthusiasm with Jennifer.

"Down, Phoebe, down! Hey, Grandpa!"

"Niffer! You're *glorious*!"

Part of her knew that grandfathers always said things like that, and part of her guessed that her father was smart enough to coach his dad on her state of mind, but most of her could tell Grandpa Crawford really meant it. She beamed.

"Goodness, Jon, will you look at her!" Crawford leapt over the porch railing, eschewing the steps, and landed right next to Jennifer. "She's a perfect blend! Hasn't been anything like her for centuries, I'll bet. Dash, trample, creep—it's all there!"

He was poking at her with a wing claw now. A bit flattered, and a little taken aback at the prodding, she grinned and waved his wing away with her own. "Did you just call me a creep?"

"Wait until you start your lessons!" he went on. "There's so much for you to learn, and to do! And we've got to get you to Crescent Valley!"

"Slow down, Dad," Jonathan interrupted with something like alarm. "She's nowhere near ready for Crescent Valley yet. There's a long road ahead for her. And if I recall correctly, you didn't let *me* enter Crescent Valley until I was sixteen years old."

"*You* were an idiot." Crawford winked.

"I've already learned a ton, Grandpa—how to fly, how to breathe fire, how to catch sheep, even how to fish!" Her own excitement sounded strange to her, as if she were a five-year-old who had just finished reading her first book all by herself.

"Wonderful!" he laughed. "I'm sorry I missed it."

It didn't matter to her that she had never seen him in this shape before—his voice, his manner, everything about him was exactly as she remembered. She almost wanted to ask him to read her a story, so she could curl up in his lap.

"I've made spaghetti sauce," Elizabeth offered from just inside the patio doors. "Don't worry, Dad, it's your family's recipe."

"That's no guarantee," Crawford muttered to Jennifer. "All right then," he said more loudly. "Bring it on out, and we'll have at it!"

Jennifer had to admit that one of the better things about being a dragon was the absolute discard of all conventional manners. Her mother brought out three large pots and simply set them on the porch. Each dragon then settled down next to a pot, and stuck his or her head in. Their slurps and gurgles were almost comic, but Jennifer was too caught up in the aroma of the sauce to care.

"This isn't bad at all, Lizzard!" Crawford belched. The nickname made Jennifer snort. She hadn't heard that one before. "You sure my son didn't help?"

Elizabeth settled down with her own neat bowl of pasta and sauce onto the only chair on the porch. Her smile betrayed both amusement and irritation. "I can follow a recipe just fine. I can also do many other things, all of which are a bit more important than cooking pitch-perfect meals for your son on a regular basis."

Crawford raised his sauce-covered jaws from his pot. To Jennifer, he looked a bit like a dinosaur peering up from a fresh kill to look over a challenger. "Now, now, *Doctor,* there's no need to get testy. I didn't mean anything by it."

There was silence for a while. Jonathan raised his head from his own pot and gave them both warning looks. Confused, Jennifer stopped chewing and let some noodles hang out of her mouth. She had never noticed this sort of tension between her mother and her grandfather before.

Her mother finally shrugged her shoulders. "Whatever. Your son cooks well enough for both of us, so it's not an issue. We won't starve anytime soon."

This seemed to break the tension. Everyone began eating again, so Jennifer followed suit. She was just licking the last bits of sauce out of the still-hot pot when the tremors began.

"Dad . . ." She couldn't control her claws, her wings, her entire body. Shaking from snout to tail, she took a few steps back as she felt her insides swirl. It was a slightly different feeling from the first change, but similar enough that Jennifer became scared. She knew what was coming—her spine, her skin, her teeth, everything would start to hurt again.

But five days ago, she had been alone. This time, her family was present and ready.

"It's okay, Jennifer." Her mother's voice soothed her. "It won't hurt so much this time. I put something in your sauce to relieve the pain."

"Something in her sauce?" Jennifer heard her grandfather ask. His voice sounded disapproving, but that could have just been the echoes inside her head. Her vision began to blur.

She heard her father, far away. "We didn't exactly talk about this, Liz . . ."

"Doctor's orders," her mother replied, farther off.

The voices continued, but Jennifer couldn't make out what they were saying anymore. Her insides were still sliding about and rubbing against each other. She could feel the same disturbing changes in her backbone and skull, only this time in reverse—and with nearly no pain at all, just mild discomfort.

"Whad did hoo pud in he sawce, Mom?" Her voice seemed tinny and miles away to her own ears. "Morfeeeene?"

She felt her body slump over as the morphine, or whatever it was, took full effect. Through the blurs before her eyes, she saw the shapes of her father and grandfather, but couldn't read their expressions.

"Grea ressipee, Mom," she said with a grin, falling asleep.

The dream was very short.

She was looking in a mirror. Her body was too thin. Visible bones slid beneath her skin as her dragon jaws and wings finished receding. There was suddenly a lump in her throat, and then a bulge in her mouth. She spit it out into her hand.

It was her second heart, the one she had felt when she had been looking at *Grayheart's Anatomy* a few days ago. The slimy, red mess was still beating in her hand . . . *da-da-thump, da-da-thump, da-da-thump* . . .

When she woke up, she was in bed. The softness of the mattress surprised her. *Too used to rugs on floors,* she chided herself. She sat up and looked around.

It was one of the guest rooms upstairs in Grandpa Crawford's cabin. The windows were ajar—the cold autumn air cut into her fragile skin—and the door to the hallway was wide open. She could just make out her family's low-key voices, probably downstairs.

There was a glass of ginger ale and a slice of lightly buttered toast on the nightstand next to her. That was a clear signal in the Scales family. She stayed in bed, reached out with her pinkish human hands, and grabbed the "sick person food." The dishes were heavier than she expected, and she almost dropped the glass. As she ate, more questions swirled through her mind.

How long had the transformation taken? Would it always hurt? Would her mother always be at her side, ready with painkilling drugs? And where the hell was her tail?

That last question was ridiculous, of course: She didn't have a tail anymore. From the moment she had woken up, she had known she was a girl again. But at the same time, she missed the tail. She hadn't thought about it much while she was a dragon, but making the tail swish behind her had been a source of comfort to her.

Relax, she told herself. *You don't need a tail. You're normal again.*

Of course, another part of her mind held firmly to the

idea that she wasn't normal at all, and wouldn't be ever again.

The voices downstairs got a bit closer—definitely her mother and father. Jennifer could hear multiple footsteps up the stairs. They were talking about the ride home, and whether Phoebe had eaten yet, and what supplies they needed to keep here for next time.

For next time. Half of Jennifer looked forward to it. Half dreaded it.

She put the empty ginger ale glass back on the night-stand and settled back down into bed. An urge to close her eyes and pretend to be asleep washed over her, but that made no sense. So when her parents entered the doorway, she was staring at the ceiling.

"How do you feel?" her father asked. He wasn't a dragon anymore, either. Two legs, no wings, no horns, thinning hair. Just like any other dad. Had it all been a stupid dream? Had they been on vacation as a human family, and the dragon parts were all one long nightmare?

"My feet are a bit numb," she replied. "My stomach's rolling a bit. And my nose itches like crazy," she realized suddenly, reaching up to scratch it.

"The numbness is from the return metamorphosis," he explained. "The other stuff is from the morphine."

"Having a six-inch horn on my snout probably didn't help, either," she complained, still scratching.

"Any difficulty breathing?"

Jennifer took a deep breath and let it out. "Nope."

"Good. Your mother and I think we should all be ready to go in about an hour. The moon's waxing, so it'll be a few weeks before our next morph. You've got school to-morrow, and your mother's got surgeries scheduled. I'll be glad to swing by the office for a day or two, myself."

Jonathan Scales was an architect. He did just about all of his work from home when he wasn't on a "business trip." Since he could pick and choose clients, he could make his work fit an unconventional schedule. His job made complete sense to Jennifer now—as did the phone in the downstairs kitchen with the oversized push-buttons and speakerphone feature.

"I think I could be ready to go in an hour," Jennifer ventured without a smile.

"The clothes you were wearing last Thursday are in the wash," her mother explained. "I brought some other stuff up for you to wear. You'll find it in the dresser."

"Thanks, Mom."

"Next time, you may want to set your clothes aside before you morph," her father suggested. "It doesn't hurt what you wear, but getting the smell of smoke, fish, and blood out afterward is a bit of a chore."

"Right. Sorry, didn't know that."

There was an awkward silence. Then her parents smiled nervously and closed the door so she could be alone.

Getting up and getting dressed was much harder than Jennifer expected. For one, the early October breeze slipping into the room chilled her fragile skin. So she tried to get over to the window to close it, and then found out that walking on legs again was like stepping on stilts.

The dresser was closer than the window, so she decided to get dressed instead. The top drawer wouldn't respond to her feeble tugs at first, but she finally managed to get it open and reach in with fumbling fingers. She wasn't sure how the jeans and sweatshirt her mother had carefully folded into the drawer would fit her. Every limb felt too long and lanky. The dragon shape had been muscular and powerful. This shape felt like one of those overly thin, pasty aliens with warped hands and feet, big bulging head and eyes.

And no tail. Tail had helped with balance.

She stumbled forward onto the bed and decided to dress lying down.

By the time she got everything on (it all fit fine), she figured she had regained enough coordination to stand up again. She slowly rose and stepped over to the mirror on the far wall to look at herself for the first time.

A sad, tired teenager stared back. Her shoulders were slumped, her weight was on one foot, and her fingers were anxiously twisting her stringy hair. There were more silver streaks in her hair than before, but it wasn't shiny like it sometimes was.

"I should have taken a shower," her reflection said aloud. Jennifer couldn't have agreed more.

The ride home was quiet and uneventful. Phoebe snuggled up next to Jennifer on the backseat of the minivan for most of the way, occasionally licking her ear. Once in a while, one parent or the other would ask her a question about how she felt, or whether she had enjoyed seeing Grandpa again (she had, though seeing his human form that morning had reminded her how old he truly was), or if she still had homework to do.

Jennifer answered all of these with the fewest words possible. Noncommittal grunts were her favorite. She knew these drove her mom and dad nuts, but she didn't care. *Who has a normal conversation after something like this past week,* she asked herself. Nobody came to mind.

*   *   *

The next dream took Jennifer a bit by surprise, since it didn't happen at night, but rather on the school bus the following morning. Eddie wasn't at the bus stop like he usually was in the morning, so she was riding alone.

As she stared out the bus window, she began to see the strangest farm animals.

Skinny horses, with joints almost protruding from their hides, walking down the street and driving cars. Plump pigs, with legs practically disappearing under folds of tender flesh, clustered together at bus stops. Stringy chickens, most with only a few feathers, crossing the road in jumps and starts.

Then she felt a poke on her shoulder. She turned and pulled back in surprise. Two tall and thin sheep stood in the aisle. Each had impossibly long legs, with strange joints that shook with the vibrations of the accelerating bus. One rested a fragile, spindly hoof on the seat by her neck. It leaned forward and stared at her with two bulging black eyes.

"This seat taken?" It said in a familiar voice.

Jennifer shook her head and rubbed her eyes. When she looked back up, the sheep were gone, as well as all the other farm animals on the bus. Skip stood in front of her instead, with his sly grin.

"Nope. Have a seat," she said with a mixture of relief and caution. She dreaded trying to explain her absence to Skip, although her parents had worked out an elaborate story of tragic illness.

But Skip didn't press her much. "Say, you feeling okay? Ms. Graf told us you were sick."

"Yeah, sick," she mumbled. She tried to change the topic. "So I've never seen you get on the bus before. Your family's house is around here?"

He shifted uncomfortably in his seat. "My aunt sold it to Dad, yeah. Since Mom died . . ."

The uncomfortable silence lay on them for a while. Jennifer didn't want to talk about her illness, and Skip clearly didn't want to talk about his dead mother. Finally, she took a deep breath.

"So, seen Eddie lately?"

That worked fine. Skip set in on a string of topics ranging from how he and Eddie had spent all weekend playing catch to how much homework they had gotten in Ms. Graf's class and whether Jennifer would ever catch up.

But Jennifer discovered as she listened that she didn't much care if she caught up, or fell further behind, or ever graduated from Winoka High. With every word of Skip's that passed through one ear and out the other, she felt more and more that coming to school at all anymore was pointless.

She knew how to read and write. She could do math better than some college students. History never interested her. And science? Her admiration of her mother's career would remain that—admiration, bounded by the very real limits that getting "chronically, terminally ill" would present to a fourteen-year-old. So why was she here? What possible use was school to a creature like her?

Running her hand through her hair, she felt disgust at touching the graying strands. For every moment she had spent hating her dragon body the week before, she hated this one more. This biped thing she had going on seemed wrong somehow. And how could that be, when she'd only been a dragon for a few days, but had walked around on two miserable, pale legs all her life?

Skip didn't seem to notice her inattention. In fact, he kept talking to her as the bus finally reached the school and they all got off. Apparently, he took her silence and occasional eye contact as approval to talk nonstop. As Jennifer got off the bus, she almost keeled over with the stress the steps gave her body. She muffled a desperate chuckle. The star athlete of her class, and she could hardly stand to be in her own skin!

She marched through the first couple of classes in a daze. One time in the hallway she passed Susan, but her friend seemed uncomfortable even looking at her. Jennifer guessed this was probably for the best.

In the classroom, she didn't talk, no matter how hard her teachers tried to engage her. When Ms. Graf tried to make an issue of it in science, Jennifer fixed her with glassy, contemptuous gray eyes. Ms. Graf returned a withering look for the rudeness, but left Jennifer alone for the rest of the period.

The bell rang and the class filed out. Jennifer once again lapsed into a stream of sour thoughts, broken suddenly by Bob Jarkmand's loud, "S'matter, Scabs? You seem all pissed off. You got *girly* problems?"

Girly problems. Ovulation. Reproduction. Bob's brief interruption set Jennifer thinking again. What kind of kid would she have, years from now? It had always seemed weird to guess at before, but now the very thought of it made her sick to her stomach. Of course, thinking of sex and children—

"Look at her, she's all freaked out by her girly problems. I bet that's what happens when you lose your virginity and start slutting around the school . . ."

—was beside the point. There was no way she was putting a kid of her own through this. *Nope, sorry, everybody off the genetic train, time's up*. She would enjoy her life as a lizard-spinster-hermit—

"Don't talk to her like that, punk!"

That broke her train of thought. Skip had stomped up to within a few feet of Bob. The nearby students all stopped talking to look. Bob wasn't much taller than Skip, but he was far broader. Unlike the last time they sparred, there were no teachers or classroom chairs to get in the way. *How sweet,* thought Jennifer watching Skip's direct challenge. *Suicidal, but sweet.* She offered him a grim smile, but he was busy staring down the larger boy.

"Don't ever talk to her," Skip continued. "Don't you even look at her."

"Why, *Francis*? You her boyfriend for the day? Lotsa luck. Scabs seems like the kind of girl who likes to get around. She'll be hangin' with someone else tomorrow, I bet." Bob stepped forward, putting Skip entirely in his shadow. "In fact, I *know* she will. Because you'll be in the hospital."

Abruptly, Jennifer ran out of patience. It was charming of Skip to help and all, but . . .

She stepped forward and slammed Bob right across the face with her fist. The *crack* made the surrounding crowd gasp and from all the way down the hall heads turned. Even more, the shot knocked Bob off his feet and a couple of yards to the left, where he hit the wall by the guidance counselor's office with a satisfying *whoomph*. He slid to the floor and rolled across the doorway. A quick hand clapped to his mouth, but not before Jennifer saw blood spurt through his split lips.

Skip stared at the fallen thug, then at Jennifer. He crouched and shook a finger in Bob's face. "And there's plenty more where that came from, buster!"

Jennifer waved her hand, expecting it to hurt from the punch—but it didn't.

"Humiliating," Skip said cheerfully, "yet exhilarating. So much for my knight in shining armor routine, eh? Amazing punch, Jenny—I mean, Jennifer! Wow! I'll . . ." His eyes got a little wider as he stared past Jennifer. "I'll . . . um . . . see you later."

"Why, where are you going?"

"You should worry about where *you're* going, young lady." A hand closed over her shoulder. She knew without turning that it was the reclusive guidance counselor, Mr. Pool. He must have stepped over Bob to get out of his office. "You're in a lot of trouble."

"*She's* in trouble?" Skip's look was incredulous, and he pointed to the bully plastered on the floor. "*He* started it."

Mr. Pool's oily eyes rested on the new kid. "You may not be familiar with the code of conduct at this high school yet, Mr. Wilson," he hissed, "but you will be soon. It includes showing respect to your elders."

"I'll show respect for those elders that deserve it," Skip shot back.

Jennifer wasn't sure what to do here. The solution last time had involved a straight punch to the jaw; but somehow that seemed less appropriate this time around. She didn't have time to figure it all out: Mr. Pool decided to drag her away without further comment. She saw Skip fix a hot glare at the back of the counselor's neck as Pool dragged her off.

"I don't mind saying I'm shocked! According to her records, Jennifer never had any sort of disciplinary problems before high school." The principal of Winoka High School, Mr. Mouton, settled down behind his desk after shaking both Jonathan's and Elizabeth's hands, and motioning them to take the two vinyl chairs in front of him. Jennifer chewed her tongue in an uncomfortable fiberglass chair off to one side.

"Mr. Mutton—" Jonathan began.

"That's *Moo-TONE,* if you please. May I add, Mr. and Mrs. Scales, it's nice to meet you both. Though the circumstances could be better, of course. As the new principal here, I've been trying to meet parents before there's a problem. I wish we could have done so in this case. My assistant tells me she's had trouble scheduling a time when Mr. Scales is available . . . ?"

Jennifer shot an accusing look at her father, and then a triumphant one at her mother. *HA!*

"I'm usually on the road," Jonathan explained slowly. "Elizabeth has been in closer contact with Jennifer's schools, as a rule."

"Hmmm."

"We're both very interested in Jennifer's education, Mr. Mouton. But schedules sometimes . . ."

"It hasn't hurt her academic performance one bit," the principal interrupted congenially. "At least not yet. But these years are usually the point when the rules change, Mr. and Mrs. Scales."

Elizabeth shifted uncomfortably in her seat. Jonathan got the signal. "My wife makes every parent-teacher conference, soccer game, and art fair. And I make such events when I can. We've always supported Jennifer—"

"Yes, of course, of course." It was a concession and a dismissal at the same time. Mr. Mouton ruffled some papers and produced a file. It was rather thin, but he fanned through the skimpy pages as though he were thumbing through a dictionary. "It's not unusual in these cases, Mr. and Mrs. Scales, for a child to act out in the absence of her parents. You say you spend lots of time on the road. Jennifer *may* have been calling for your attention."

"Or she *may* have been calling the school bully on his atrocious behavior."

Jennifer nearly fell out of her chair. Her *mother* had said that! Not only did Elizabeth seem to know about Bob Jarkmand already, she was taking sides—*her* side!

The principal's cheeks grew rosy. "Be that as it may, Mrs. Scales—"

"That's Dr. Georges-Scales, if you please. Why isn't the thug in here answering questions?" Elizabeth looked up and down the principal's office, obviously expecting to see the largest boy at Winoka High strung up next to the diplomas and awards on the paneled wall.

"The 'thug,' as you put it, is in the nurse's office, chewing ice chips in an attempt to get the swelling down," Mouton said coolly. "No matter what Robert said to Jennifer, violence is not the answer."

"Save your platitudes. I see the consequences of violence every day, and I know the type that breeds it. I understand this Robert was not only talking at my daughter as if she were a whore, but also threatening one of her friends. Did you talk to this witness?"

"Not yet," admitted Mr. Mouton. Jennifer could see from her mother's expression that she already knew the answer. Skip had caught her parents on the way into the principal's office, then, and told them everything. *He skipped class to lurk outside the office and talk to them.* Jennifer smiled to herself. *Knight in shining armor, indeed!*

Mr. Mouton caught the smile and turned on her. "This is not a laughing matter, Ms. Scales."

Jennifer didn't drop the corners of her mouth. "I can't help what I find funny."

"Best you keep quiet, dear," Elizabeth snapped. The warm mother-daughter relationship dissipated instantly.

"Why should I stay quiet?" she snapped back. "You're all talking about me. About *my* life. About how *I'm* stuck here at this pointless school for *no reason at all.*"

Elizabeth ignored the rant. "Mr. Mouton. Last week, our daughter was diagnosed with a rather serious medical condition. While the tests are not yet conclusive, it appears . . ."

"I'M A FREAK!" Jennifer stood up and screamed at Mr. Mouton, startling the man against the back of his worn vinyl chair. "I'M A FREAK AND THERE IS NO CURE! I GET IT FROM MY FATHER, AND MY GRANDFATHER! WE'RE ALL FREAKS, BUT I'M A BIT MORE OF A FREAK! CONCENTRATED FREAK! FREAK WITH SPECIAL NEW AND IMPROVED FREAKY-FEATURES!"

Jonathan got up quickly and braced an arm around her. Gently but firmly, he pushed her back down into the chair. His voice was too soft for anyone beyond Jennifer to hear.

"If you continue," he breathed, "we will *ground* you."

Ground had a new twist on it. No flying? No fishing? Chained up in the cabin basement, souped up on morphine and bad samples of her mother's cooking?

She fumed silently.

Jonathan turned to Mr. Mouton. "I think if you put together what my wife and my daughter are saying, you'll see that discipline in this case is neither completely warranted nor necessary. I'd appreciate it if you would let us handle this within the family. Due to certain . . . issues . . . regarding Jennifer's health we had . . . her mother and I had discussed the possibility of homeschooling. Perhaps the time has come to do more than talk about it."

Mr. Mouton rubbed his chin thoughtfully, trying to show how well he had recovered from Jennifer's outburst. "Well . . . I could talk to the Jarkmands. Given Robert's record, it shouldn't be too hard to show them both sides of the story. I can't guarantee they'll drop the matter, but Jennifer's condition . . . speaking of which, I don't want to seem insensitive, but, er, it would help if we had some documentation of . . . er . . ."

"I'll sign a doctor's note *myself.*" Elizabeth rolled her eyes. "Heaven forbid a school principal should pick his own nose without a signed doctor's note."

"We're going now," Jonathan announced. Gripping his daughter's collar and his wife's wrist, he began a hasty exit. "Thank you, Mr. Mouton . . ."

"*Mouton . . .*" Jennifer managed to resist her father's momentum long enough to stare into her school principal's eyes. "Mr. Dejarnais in French class taught us that means *sheep,* right?"

"That's right," Mr. Mouton replied uncertainly.

Before she could say anything else, she was pulled through the office doorway with a squawk.

CHAPTER 7

The Farm Under Crescent Moon

"I've never thought this about you before, Jennifer," her father hissed once they were in the car and headed home, "but either you're not nearly as smart as we've always thought, or you don't care whether your family lives or dies."

"Oh come on, Dad! Mouton's a dork, and I was just having a little fun—"

"This is not a game!" He was shouting into the rearview mirror. "There are enemies—things you've never even heard of—that would cut my head off in an instant if they knew what I was. Yours, too."

"That doesn't sound so bad," she pouted. "I hate living like this, anyway." Looking out the backseat window, she spotted a black-haired ram in a suit, holding hooves with a scrawny blonde ewe in a floral print dress. A trio of fluffy lambs wove in and out of their path on the sidewalk. She rubbed her eyes, but the animal shapes were still there when she looked again. . . . This was getting worse. . . .

Her father went on. "We had hoped that you could have attended school for a few days, before pulling you out for 'medical' reasons. Missing school like you did last week, coming back for one day, and then disappearing overnight again will look suspicious. And then on top of that—on top of that!—you punch out an enormous kid like Bob Jarkmand. He may have deserved it, but a hall-way boxing match is hardly compatible with a tale of chronic and debilitating sickness!"

"Maybe you can just say I'm mentally ill," she sneered. "I feel like I'm going crazy anyway!"

The expression in the rearview mirror softened, but only slightly. "Of course you're not crazy, Jennifer. And we're trying not to land too hard on you, here—"

"You could have fooled me."

"—but you need to use your head!"

She sniffed and wiped away tears in time to see a Jersey cow driving a minivan by them. Several peach piglets were strapped in the backseats. "I'm sorry I can't get every detail of being a dragon down exactly right the first time."

Elizabeth cut in. "Being a teenager while this is hap-pening can't be easy. But whether we understand your pain or not, you've got to listen to your father. He's trying to tell you there are codes of behavior. When you break those codes, you put us all in danger. So you need to grow up."

The way her mother inserted herself into this conver-sation infuriated Jennifer. She glared at the back of her parents' heads. "In other words, this is a big vaudeville show, I'm your puppet, and you're both annoyed that I'm not moving and talking the way I'm supposed to with an arm jammed up my wooden butt!"

* * *

They had not cared for that last clever metaphor at all, Jennifer reflected later in the quiet isolation of her room. Her posters of boy bands, soccer stars, and fantasy movies were on the floor in tatters. She was sketching an endless flock of sheep with her charcoal stick directly on the faded pink wall. Across their backs, she suggested a dark, winged shadow.

"Jennifer?"

She didn't turn around. "Come on in, Susan. Skip and Eddie can come in, too. Make sure they know not to put weight on that top bit of the trellis."

"What are you doing?" Susan sounded worried as the boys scrambled over the sill behind her.

"Who keeps their window open in Novem— Hey!" Eddie's voice was even more concerned than Susan's, but he tried to joke. "Won't your parents execute you for doing that? My Dad caught me with crayons on the wall when I was four, and I can still remember the court-martial."

Jennifer still didn't turn around. "They won't punish me. I won't be spending much time in this room, anyway. And I figured you would be coming—that's why I left the window open. Please close it, Skip."

She heard the window close, then Susan's tentative voice. It was difficult to pay attention: She could smell food. *Prey?* Her better sense chased the thought away.

Susan was saying that Skip had told her and Eddie about what happened with Bob Jarkmand, and that Bob had to go to the hospital, and the whole school was talking. That, and maybe Jennifer wasn't coming back to school, because she had been expelled . . .

"That's not true," Jennifer interrupted.

Susan paused. "No? Then what happened?"

"I'm not expelled. I'm . . ." It was so hard to lie to her friends like this. "I don't want to talk about it."

"Skip was saying he heard maybe you were really sick, which makes sense," offered Eddie. "I mean, the way you jumped out of my dad's truck last week. If you don't want to talk about it, that's cool. But please don't feel alone. We're here if you need us."

Jennifer reached out behind her and grabbed Eddie's knee as he crouched down by her. "Thanks, Eddie."

They all breathed out with a bit of relief before she continued. "But this feels like a solo run, guys. At least for now. You can stay if you like. Put on some music, make yourselves at home. Heck, pick up a stick of charcoal if you want. But I won't be talking too much."

"I don't get it," Susan said, ignoring what Jennifer just said. "The championship wasn't that long ago! You played great. That kick! And then hitting Bob in the hallway—you seem so strong. How can you be sick?"

Jennifer stood and began sketching trees off in the distance, far away from the sheep. No cover for the poor little sheep.

Her friend tried again. "Anyway, I acted like a jerk today when I didn't even say hello. I couldn't figure out what to say. I'm really sorry. I mean, you're my best friend, and we haven't seen or talked to each other in a long time. I miss you."

Jennifer couldn't bring herself to speak. Part of her was thrilled that Susan still cared, but most of her wished she had locked her window and avoided this. Why become best friends again, when she'd just have to disappear again before the next crescent moon—possibly for good?

A moment passed, and then Susan exploded. "Dammit, could you at least turn around and *look* at us?"

I'm afraid of the shapes I might see, Jennifer thought. She remembered the spindly sheep on the bus, and the animals all over town. She liked her friends the way she remembered them, not stretched out like some kind of insane claymation farm movie characters. But she didn't know how to put her fear into words.

"This is getting old fast," snarled Susan.

"Susan, cut her a break!" pleaded Eddie. "We can't know what it's—"

"I had a mother who was sick, five years ago." Susan interrupted. "I'm sure Jennifer remembers her. She died six months after the doctors discovered her cancer. She spent those six months wrapped up in her own pain, not talking to anyone. Not even me, though I stayed by her bed night after night. She got thinner and thinner in that bed. Barely a word all that time. And then she died, without making it right. It was selfish and cruel.

"If Jennifer wants to do this, fine. But I'm not wasting any more time here. It hurts too much to watch."

Jennifer heard scraping at the window, which apparently was stuck closed now, then a slam on the sill. "Fine, screw the window. I'll go out the front door."

As Susan opened the door and passed into the hall, Jennifer caught a glimpse of her friend—a midnight-black Arabian galloping by, with glitter in its mane and long, velvety cheeks streaked with blush and tears. Jennifer set aside the image and remembered Susan's mother. How stupid of her to forget! She should never have let her parents use illness as an excuse.

She wanted badly to call out, but now matters were worse. How would Susan feel if she found out that Jennifer and her family were using a wasting disease as some sort of neat and convenient cover story?

It didn't matter. This was inevitable. She'd lose all of them. Not all right away, but one by one . . .

"Susan!" Eddie rushed out of the room, in the shape of a silver stallion. "Jennifer, I'll get her. Susan!"

There were footsteps on stairs, and mumbled voices, and Susan shouting, and then her parents' voices, too. Then Susan shouting again and a door slamming. Then silence.

She waited for a moment.

"Skip, if you're staying, pick up some charcoal."

"Okay." She made out his shape out of the corner of her eye as he bent over, picked up a stick, and reached up with another hand to pull down one of the lingering posters on her wall. "You want more sheep, or something else?"

"Something else," she said, shuddering. In her waking dream, she saw once more in his place the spindly sheep-creature from the bus. It was all she could do not to look at it directly as it pawed at her wall with graceless appendages. "Definitely something else, now. I don't care what."

Jennifer stopped eating the next day. Ever since the meeting with Mr. Mouton, she felt too predatory—she found herself craving meals too much and feeling guilty that everyone around her seemed to take on the shape, smell, or surname of a tasty snack. Of course, not eating made the cravings worse, and before the week was out, Jennifer saw food in the most alarming places—noodles in the bathroom sink drain, sugar cookies lacing the windows, and fish flopping around the dirty clothes strewn all over her floor.

She hardly left her room for three weeks, letting her mother bring her food she would not eat—she tried a bit of chicken soup once, and spit it out when it tasted like blood—and plead with her to sip water and nibble on bread. She covered her walls in charcoal—the flocks of sheep were now hunted by droves of vengeful angels and (where Skip had injected his own artistic taste) a couple of black, faceless butterflies. He had left enough pink from the wall showing through their wings that they looked a bit like that Swordtail that Jennifer had heard screaming in Ms. Graf's class weeks ago—years ago, it seemed now.

Skip and Eddie came to see her every couple of days after school, sometimes together, sometimes apart. They invariably brought up food that Jennifer's parents hoped she would eat if offered by different hands, and then ate it themselves when the ploy didn't work.

More often than not, they appeared in their strange shapes—Eddie as a beautiful silver stallion with brown speckles, and Skip as a pair of overly tall and skinny sheep. Neither distortion was comforting to Jennifer, so she usually turned away, complaining that she needed to rest her eyes, and let them talk about high school ("boring"), and Bob Jarkmand ("healing"), and even girls they thought were cute ("giggling").

If the topic was mundane enough, she would ask a question or two, just to keep them talking. After all, even if they would leave like Susan someday, she wasn't ready to lose everybody at once. And perhaps after enough talk, a corner of Jennifer's mind insisted, she could find some way to tell them the truth after all.

But the time was never right in those weeks after Susan left. Whenever Eddie or Skip turned the conversation to her or her condition, Jennifer would tighten and shake her head. They knew then to drop the subject.

One early morning, hours before sunrise, someone she had barely seen for two weeks woke her up: her father.

"We're going," he said simply.

"Where?"

"Grandpa's farm. Get dressed."

The idea of going to the farm during a crescent moon was enough to pique Jennifer's interest. She had considered refusing to move during her next morph, just to have Skip the Sheep and Eddie the Horse walk in one day and find Jennifer the Dragon in her bed! But that could wait.

"Will any other weredragons be there?"

"Get dressed. Remember, no good clothes."

He drove her up to the cabin himself, as the waning crescent moon drifted off to the east. Despite Jennifer's protests, he did not let Phoebe come with them.

"There won't be time to play with your dog. Your mother's staying home. They'll look after each other."

And so they went up alone, in a quiet drive that seemed longer than it actually was. By the time they got to the cabin, Jennifer began to feel both excited and nervous—she saw the wildflower fields she had flown over, and the wrecked beehive, and the sheep (*real* sheep, not skinny-Skip-sheep) lying in the pasture.

"You got any of that morphine Mom used last time?" she asked her father nervously as he parked the minivan.

He glanced out of the corner of his eye. "I don't exactly approve of your mother's methods. There's a lot about being a weredragon she can't understand. Most of what you felt that first night was fear, not pain."

"That's funny. It felt an awful lot like back-bending, brain-cooking pain. Yep, now that I think of it, that's what it was."

"It won't be so bad this time. The more the change happens, the more you get used to it. Taking morphine, or anything else, just means it'll take longer for you to adjust."

Nothing—not even the wind, nor the golden eagles she had seen daily on their last visit—made any movement or sound around them in the dusk. Her father got out of the minivan, lifted the back door, and pulled out the bags they had packed. "You didn't pack enough, but your mother can bring up more clothes for you, in a week or so."

"How long are we going to stay here?"

"For a while. Your mother and I decided—"

"*You and Mom* decided?"

"—that it's simply too dangerous to let you wander around Winoka, where you might make a mistake—"

"What do you mean, make a mistake?"

"—and beyond that, we're concerned for your health, since you haven't been eating—"

"*I* can decide what I eat and when!"

"—so anyway, you need to stay someplace for as long as it takes."

"For as long as it takes for what? For someone to actually seek *my* input on *my* own future?"

"For as long as it takes for you to get comfortable with who you are now."

She followed him up through the barn and into the connecting mudroom. "Comfortable with who I am! I'm *never* going to be comfortable with who I am! I hate that

I don't look like you or Grandpa. I hate the way it changes the way I see and smell things. I hate the way it makes me lie to my friends. And I hate how much it hurts." She flopped down on an armchair in the sitting room. Her father paused in the doorway to the kitchen long enough to look at her.

"This is why you need this time. Trust me, Jennifer."

"I can't trust someone who's been lying to me for fourteen years," she spat. Once it was out, she didn't want to take it back. It felt too much like the truth.

He stared at her but didn't reply. Instead, he went into the kitchen.

The change came less than an hour later, and as much as Jennifer hated to admit it, her father was right. It didn't hurt as much as it had the first time. Her insides still twisted uncomfortably, and the way her spine crinkled still creeped her out beyond belief, but there was little pain in her jaws, claws, or limbs.

With less pain and fear, Jennifer was able to observe her own transformation more clearly. The most interesting part, she told herself while gritting her teeth through the modest aches, was the unfolding of the wings. A sheath burst out of her shoulder blades and wrapped itself around arms and torso. It spun out the thin material that stretched from her scaly wrist to her glistening abdomen. Then her elbows bent backward with a sickening *grapp*, though it felt to her like little more than cracking her knuckles.

All in all, she couldn't decide which was the more troubling—the first change weeks ago, when she was terrified and could barely see anything, or this one, where she knew what was happening and could calmly observe the dragon shape obliterating her human body.

As the tint of electric blue came to her thickening skin and the greasy horn began to poke out of her elongated snout, she finally decided it sucked either way.

Her father came in from the kitchen when they had both morphed—he had given her some privacy, at her request—and looked her over with a smile that fell short of his silver eyes. The comment she had made earlier apparently stuck with him.

"The moon's been coming out of last quarter for at least a day. The others will be here soon. Wait here."

"What, you're leaving?"

His silver eyes held an icy tint. "Don't pretend to be disappointed."

Jennifer had never experienced bitterness from her own father, and it surprised her. It made him seem a lot younger—or perhaps herself a lot older. A surge of guilt flushed her cheeks.

"I'm sorry I've been acting so difficult—"

"Don't be sorry," he interrupted, holding her gaze. "You're right to feel the way you feel. But I think I am doing more harm than good. Your grandfather will be a better tutor for you."

"Where will you go? I mean, you're a dragon, Dad. Shouldn't you stay here, at least for the crescent moon?"

"I'll go where I often go when I'm like this. Crescent Valley."

"Can I—I mean, after a while, do you think I could go there, too?"

He paused and for the second time in the conversation, revealed an expression she had never seen before. This time, it was as if he was weighing her with his eyes, or examining her for faults. It made her feel both resentful and anxious at once.

"In time," he finally said. "For now, I've got to get moving while there's still enough moonlight on the water." He turned to leave.

"When will I see you again?" She felt herself start to panic. What if Grandpa didn't come? What if the other weredragons were unfriendly? And what did moonlight on the water have to do with anything?

"I'll probably stay there a few weeks," he said. "Your mother's going to be out of town on seminars. I'll pick up the van on the way back."

"Wait, weeks? I thought you only stayed in dragon shape while the crescent moon lasted."

He leaned in close and bared his sharp teeth in a mysterious smile. "Curious, isn't it?"

And then, with a rush of wind, he was gone.

Sunrise came about an hour later, and there was still no sign of anyone else. Silence and the dewy scent of dawn lay in the crisp October air. Jennifer curled up on the porch and waited, looking over her nose horn for any sign of anyone and wondering if she ought to catch something to eat for herself . . . when suddenly breakfast came to her.

Half a dozen of Grandpa's sheep, far away from their grazing pastures, came lumbering around the northeast corner of the cabin. They looked terrified.

The sound of galloping feet came surging right after, and before Jennifer could react three enormous olive green shapes barged around the same corner in hot pursuit. All three dragons—for they were dragons, though not of any kind Jennifer had ever seen before—gave a boisterous roar that practically knocked her off the porch. Then, like thunderstorms in skin, they redoubled their pace and charged after their prey.

"Hey, what're you—" she began, but her voice was lost in the horrific din. Was she seeing animal shapes again, or was this real?

It was in fact real, she decided, and a real hunt at that. The predators' forearms were thick and strong, and the sparse wing webbing that connected these limbs to their bodies seemed more decorative than useful. Certainly they were more comfortable on the ground than Jennifer still was. She couldn't imagine these bulky shapes circling over a lake full of fish like her father, or diving gracefully down to pluck anything out of anywhere.

But it was their violent crimson eyes that really caught her attention. Three pairs of narrow red pinpoints sprinted toward their prey, completely focused. If the sheep had been gazelles, they wouldn't have been any better off, Jennifer was sure.

One caught up to a straggling sheep. With a quick movement of its head, it ducked under the animal's belly and gored its rib cage with a nose horn. The sheep flipped up into the air and fell dead.

Ew. She winced. With a wing claw, she fingered her own nose horn tentatively.

The other two dragons had almost caught up to their own sheep when two slender blue shapes flipped over the nearby trees and swooped down. Their scales were almost exactly the same shade as Jennifer's, but their enormous wings had patterns of pink, orange, and yellow that reminded her more of a butterfly than a dragon.

With a spirited laugh, the newcomers swung their tails

down and struck each of the green dragons with the tips. Sparks flew, and there were shouts of protest and more laughter. The blue dragons tried to get at the surviving sheep, but the green dragons would have none of it.

"Hey, Catherine!" one of the flyers giggled with flashing, golden eyes. "What's the matter? Haven't learned how to fly yet?"

"Come closer and say that" came the good-natured response. "I'll have *you* for breakfast instead."

"You're going hungry today! These sheep are ours!"

As both groups chased each other back and forth, Jennifer thought she saw a shadow by the edge of the trees move. It was a mound of dirt and weeds that she wasn't sure had ever been there before. Staring directly at it, she realized that it had eyes—silver eyes. They fixed on the sheep, and the dragons chasing them.

They looked hungry, and not entirely friendly.

CHAPTER 8

The Legend of the Ancient Furnace

Jennifer raised her head, not knowing what this mysterious mound with eyes was or whether to warn the others—but before she could even say a word, the clump struck. As an unobservant sheep trotted by, its jaws flared out, grabbed the poor thing by its fluffy neck, and twisted.

"Creeper!" one of the blue dragons cried out, but he was still laughing. "Creeper alert! Mullery's trying to horn in on our meal!"

This got all of them working together. But before green or blue dragon could reach the site of the attack, the newcomer had disappeared again, wrapping its shadowy skin around its prey somewhere in the prickly brush.

"Come out, Mullery!" they all roared, swiping gently at the branches. "Show yourself, and the sheep! Or we'll burn this forest down looking for you."

"You will *not*," Jennifer abruptly shouted, jumping

over the porch railing and landing (rather elegantly, she congratulated herself) on the lawn not far from them. They all started a bit at her interruption, but quickly smiled when they saw who she was.

"You're Crawford's granddaughter, aren't you?" said one of the olive-skinned dragons.

"That's right. I'm Jennifer Scales. Who are you, and why are you chasing our sheep around our barn and talking about burning down our forest?"

The dragon extended a wing claw. "Catherine Brandfire. We're just joking about burning the forest—we know the rules around here."

Jennifer reluctantly shook the offered claw. "All right, then. What about the sheep?"

"What, you want one? Join the hunt. But that'll mean two of us go hungry, instead of just one!" She said this last to the whole group, and there were a few chuckles.

"Why haven't I ever seen you around here before?"

Catherine shrugged. "Well, I'm pretty new. Only turned sixteen a few weeks ago. But the others have been coming here for years. Some of us get bored around mealtime—picking off prey is too easy, unless you have a bit of competition!"

A blue dragon, still hovering over their heads, broke in. "You want a challenge, Catherine? Wait until you hunt the oreams of Crescent Valley!"

"Hang on a moment. You guys come here every crescent moon? And you know my grandfather?"

"It would be hard not to!" This came from the moving clump of weeds with silver eyes, which emerged from the brush and changed color and texture rapidly to reveal a dragon shape. This one was not unlike her own father and grandfather: dark purple, with a bony forehead pulled back in a black crest. "Everyone knows Elder Scales, and his son, Jonathan." He did not smile, but there was respect in his voice.

Jennifer idly wondered what being an elder meant, but something else was bothering her right now. "How come I've never seen any of you before?"

A blue dragon with a pinkish hue on the underside of his wings landed gently next to her. "I'll bet you've never been here during a crescent moon?"

"No . . . I guess not. Not until a few weeks ago." She had never really paid attention to moon phases before all this nonsense. Why should she? She enjoyed the nighttime sky like anyone else, but she was no astronomer.

"Crawford had us leave last time, before you arrived. Your family thought it might be easier. It's nice to finally meet you, Jennifer! I'm Alex Rosespan. I've been a dasher for the last six years, and my brother, Patrick, has, too, for just a couple of months. If it weren't for your grandfather, Patrick and I wouldn't have had anywhere to go when we first morphed. This is like a second home to us."

"And for all of us," chimed in Catherine. "I've only morphed twice before, but everyone knows Crawford's farm is the safest place to be if you're a weredragon. It's also where the tutors come to show the newer arrivals how to manage their powers."

"Powers? You mean like breathing fire and flying?"

"And the more interesting stuff." Catherine's crimson eyes glowed. "Like lizard-calling for us tramplers, or camouflage for creepers like Mullery."

"This is my first year as a tutor," Alex explained. "I'll be helping dashers with their tailwork."

Jennifer sat back on her haunches, flicking her tail nervously. This all sounded suspiciously like more school. . . .

"Do you know which type you'll follow?"

"What's that?" The question made no sense.

"What type?" Alex pressed. "I mean you look like you've got a bit of everything in you—horn and build of a trampler, skin and tail of a dasher, and, of course, creeper's in your blood—and I don't know if that's ever happened before, even when families cross over. Kids with different parents favor one type or the other."

Like an unwelcome winter wind, the recollection that she was a freak among monsters slapped Jennifer's scaled cheeks and reddened them. What on earth must these perfect breeds, who all looked similar within their tidy hunting groups, think of her? It was like being a mutt among pedigrees. "I . . . um . . . I dunno. My dad didn't . . . my grandpa hasn't . . . it's because of my dumb mom . . ."

"I think it's a lovely mix," Catherine said warmly. "You're striking! And I bet crossing types will come in handy. Each breed has its strengths and weaknesses—for example, we tramplers can't fly too well. But I'll bet you can pick up whatever skills you like, and be great at them. Maybe we'll learn lizard-calling together?"

"Lizard-whuh?" She was too taken aback by the green dragon's kindness to pick up the term. "You really think I'd be any good at it?"

"Sure, why not? You never know until you try, right? I learned that when I started junior year and had to pick up calculus. Turns out I didn't fail miserably."

Jennifer wanted to hug this stranger on the spot, but suddenly a shadow landed to her left, startling her. It was Grandpa Crawford.

"Making friends already, Niffer?" he said smoothly. "Fabulous! But it's almost time for breakfast. If you others will finish your kill and bring it up to the cabin, we'll have a roast and then share some stories."

By the time breakfast began, Jennifer had counted no fewer than thirty-two different dragons running through her grandfather's pastures, or slinking through the trees, or sailing over the lake on tranquil wings. There were tramplers like Catherine, all some shade of green with large bodies, crimson eyes behind any number of nose horns, and not much in the way of wings; dashers like Alex, with small bright blue bodies, golden eyes, and brilliant patterns under their broad wings; and creepers like her father and grandfather, purple or black for the most part, horns or crests at the backs of their heads, and not often seen because of the way their scales seemed to shift color and texture at will.

It was odd, seeing her second home populated by completely foreign creatures. But the more she thought about it, the more she realized so much of what she thought familiar was changing—the people back home, her friends, her family, herself, everything.

Sheep was on the menu, of course, and Jennifer took the time to catch and prepare her own. It made her feel more like she was blending in, and she had to admit the more she saw of these other dragons, the more the idea appealed to her. Besides, she realized as she watched them hunt, she hadn't eaten solid food in days, and that seemed stupid in retrospect. What *had* she been thinking?

The dragons were a boisterous lot when they gathered. She couldn't really tell anyone's gender, nor their age, though if her parents were right, everyone would be at least a couple of years older than she. Dashers

mingled with creepers, and creepers with tramplers—
no one seemed to care much who was who, and no
dragon was alone. Even Jennifer, who was trying to sit
back and observe everyone else over her own ketchup-
splashed sheep bits, found herself laughing at jokes she
overheard, and smiling back at those who passed her on
the porch.

"Time for a story!" one of the dashers called out after
most of them had finished eating. "Where's old Crawford? Crawdad, tell us a tale!"

"I'm right here! But why doesn't anyone ever write
these things down when I tell them, so you don't have to
keep bugging me?" Her grandfather's voice was boisterous, and made the others laugh. "Very well, a story. It is
our tradition after all, especially when newer dragons are
among us. This is how our people hand down history and
legends—around a meal, and under a crescent moon. We
don't keep much in the way of libraries or archives—my
sitting room has more fiction than fact, I'm afraid—but
I'll tell you a story some say is true, and some say not.

"There was a time, centuries ago, when people accepted dragons, adapted to their presence, and even
revered them in parts of the world. Civilizations believed
dragons to bring luck, weather, or even life and death.
People changed their crops, tactics in battle, and who
they would marry, all on the whisper of a whim of a
forked tongue.

"At that time, there was a force that kept dragons vital.
We do not know much about it now except for its name:
the Ancient Furnace."

"What, you mean like a big fireplace?" This interruption came from a young-sounding dasher who sat next to
Alex. Their wing patterns were similar, and so Jennifer

guessed this was Alex's brother, Patrick. "This is a story about a dumb fireplace?!"

Crawford's own granddaughter, and the more seasoned weredragons assembled, knew how little the elder cared for interruptions in the middle of a story. But he shook the comment off, showed a thin smile, and continued.

"Whatever sort of machine it was, it filled entire caverns with its grinding and roaring, and bathed entire forests in bright blue and green flames. But these fires grew the trees, rather than consuming them. Over a thousand years ago, the Ancient Furnace forged a magical refuge for weredragons, covering Crescent Valley with moon elms suitable for our kind."

Several of the dragons nodded their heads in recognition. This was driving Jennifer nuts—what the heck was this Crescent Valley? And now "moon elms"? But she knew better than to stop her grandfather.

"One night, a tribe of werachnids crept into Crescent Valley. They had learned of the Ancient Furnace's power, and they coveted it. Using sorcery, they wove webs about the Furnace's defenses, poisoned its workings, and stole its secrets. But as they tried to escape, the Furnace ground its gears in a last blast of effort, waking up the dragons and bringing them charging.

"No werachnid made it out alive, but the Ancient Furnace's machinery was irretrievably broken. Its light dimmed, its rumblings fell silent, and soon after that, it was lost."

"Lost?" This from Patrick again.

Crawford, irritated at the second interruption, snapped. "Yes, lost, boy! As in 'never found again.' "

"Why doesn't anyone just go to the same cave where it was, and look around? Maybe we could fix it?"

"You're a bright young man," the elder said without seeming at all to mean it. "No doubt you've got a map to the Ancient Furnace's true location, and a shovel and a pick, and enough superglue and know-how to fix it right back up again!"

Jennifer was enjoying the lashing—nobody lost patience like her grandpa in midstory—but a more basic question urged her forward. "Um, Grandpa . . . what's a werachnid? I mean, weredragons, werachnids . . . how many of us werethingies are there, anyway?"

He turned to face her, but with a softer expression. "Ah. Sorry, Niffer. I've told so many of these stories over and over again, I can't remember who's heard which, anymore. Well, let's see . . . werachnids . . . yes, I think I know how to explain. Follow me, everyone."

It was a short walk down to the lakeside, where Crawford opened up a large wooden box there. Jennifer always figured it held fishing tackle or life preservers, so she was surprised when he pulled out some ceramic bowls and little plastic bags of something she couldn't make out.

"Different dragons would answer Jennifer in different ways," he said taking one bowl with a swift wing claw and scooping it into the lake. "I'll answer like this: There really is only *one* set of 'werethingies,' as you put it. Watch as I add these ingredients. . . ."

They all watched him uncertainly, even the older ones among them. He shook the contents of the first small bowl onto his claw carefully, and then scraped at the leavings for quite some time before he spoke.

"Fifty grains of salt, for the ancestors that first fought," he muttered. He tipped them into the bowl. Then he lifted the second small bowl and counted something else out onto his palm.

"Fifty seeds, to bear the fruit of future generations." These went into the bowl as well.

"Fifty minutes, for how long this answer is taking," whispered Catherine, who had settled next to Jennifer. The younger dragon snorted.

"As some of you know, fifty is a number of some significance among weredragons," explained Crawford while mixing the ingredients of the large bowl with one finger claw. "A dragon is not considered mature until he has seen fifty morphs. The oream hunts use fifty hunters from each clan. The newolves use fifty different chords to speak to us. And so on."

Jennifer felt a fresh surge of irritation. She had asked what a werachnid was, and now her grandfather was talking about oreams, and newolves, and a bunch of other things she didn't know or care about! She had a sudden insight into why her father was the way he was—it must be in the genes.

Hold on, the icy thought struck. *Does that mean* I'll *be like that when I'm older?*

Crawford's voice shook her from that horrific thought. "No one knows why fifty is the number, but fifty it is. And so this drink I have made, with fifty grains of salt and fifty seeds, is a ceremonial drink among weredragons. It honors our past, our future, and the changes in between. We drink, and we adapt. Here."

He breathed a small spurt of flame over the large bowl and then held it out to Jennifer. She took it in both claws and examined its contents. Various seeds—tiny kiwi seeds, acorns, even a peach pit—peered back from the salty water.

She brought it up to her mouth and sipped. The first thing she noticed was how difficult it was for a reptilian head to sip—the liquid dribbled past her pointed teeth and down her long, narrow chin. The second thing she noticed was that this was, essentially, hot salty water.

"Yeouch!" she squeaked, dropping the bowl.

Her grandfather sighed as he surveyed the muddy seeds at her feet. "Yes, well, anyway, tradition is important. I'm sure you all get the idea."

"Sorry," Jennifer mumbled.

He winked at her and continued. "To get back to your question on werachnids, they come from the deep past, like ourselves and our traditions. 'Fifty times fifty years ago,' we dragons say when we mean longer than anyone knows. And back then, according to legend, there was only one set of people who could change shape. They were the *mutautem*, and their exploits influenced Greek, Central American, East Asian, and Norwegian mythologies: people, who some mistook for gods, shifting from one shape to another. Each *mutauta* could change to just about any living thing—fish, bird, bear, dragon, insect, even a tree—but the copy was a poor imitation.

"That is, until the First Generation came. They were the fifty children of the most powerful *mutauta*, a woman by the name of Allucina who could turn into pure living light. Each one of Allucina's children could change into a different form—one form only, but with more accuracy and grace than their forebears. There was Brigida, the eldest and first perfect dragon; and Bruce, the first perfect spider. And Bardou the wolf, Bulbul the songbird, Bennu the eagle, Bian the sea monster, and many more whose names are lost to us now."

Jennifer tried to imagine what the call downstairs to dinner must have sounded like with all these "B" names, but she kept her thoughts to herself.

"The last child was Barbara, who took no other shape, but kept her human form.

"There was great tension between many of the children—in part because there were fifty of them, and stress was only natural. But between Brigida and Bruce, the first- and second-born, there was something deeper than dislike. The dragon was fond of flying in the open air and laughing gusts of flame. She looked darkly upon her spider brother and his preference for quiet crevices and spinning webs. In return, Bruce thought his sister to be arrogant and foolish, and he was afraid of her recklessness. Their mutual fear and distrust soon evolved into hatred.

"As children, they played unkind pranks on each other—worms tucked inside a meal, tears and burns on each other's clothing, that sort of thing. Once older, Brigida and Bruce favored traps, like exploding toys and books with poisoned pages. They enlisted the younger children in alliances, and before long the family was torn in two."

Jennifer was startled. Was this what it was like to have a brother or sister? She supposed her parents spoiled her as an only child, but it seemed vastly preferable to the alternative, even if this was just a myth.

"Allucina would not stand for this, and so she turned to her youngest, Barbara, who had not allied with either side. She gave Barbara incredible powers, and mastery over the beasts. And as Allucina died—some say Bruce poisoned his own mother—she left her youngest daughter as her sole heir to all her possessions and powers, and she named Barbara matriarch of the family.

"This did not sit well with Brigida *or* Bruce—or any of the rest of them, for that matter. After years of hatching plots and setting snares, the family finally broke out into full-blown violence—Brigida and her allies, Bruce and his, and Barbara standing alone. Brothers killed sisters and vice versa, and when all was done, there were only the three of them left.

"Brigida fled to the steepest mountains, where Barbara could not chase. Bruce slipped away into a labyrinth of shadows. And to this day, thousands of years later, their brood remain dispersed, hating the sight of the others, hoping to finish the job their ancestors left undone."

Crawford finished the story and let them sit in silence for a while.

Patrick finally spoke first. "So the werachnids are people, like us, except they change into spider form? It sounds like we could just talk to them, get to know them better. I mean it's been thousands of years. Surely they don't hate us that much anymore?"

Jennifer was sure she saw her grandfather hesitate for an instant before he nodded. "They do, Patrick. They are less human now, and more spider. Out of instinct, they still hate us. They've gathered in enough numbers over the centuries to drive us out of one home after another. The last place they destroyed was Eveningstar."

Jennifer again thought back to that fateful night when she turned five and her world turned upside down. If she closed her eyes, she could just make out the screaming of unknown beasts. . . .

"But why don't we fight back?" asked Catherine. "We *must* be stronger than them! I mean, we can fly! We can breathe fire! Spiders are small. A dragon can squash a tarantula, right? They're just bugs!"

Crawford seemed caught between a rueful smile and a

forgiving wince. "These 'bugs,' as you call them, Catherine, are not small. Not small at all.

"And while they cannot do what we can do, they have their own abilities. Centuries of hiding and trapping have honed their skills. You say we can fly? They can jump, and jump high, to catch their prey! They don't miss. They have excellent vision, and the most powerful among them can see across space and time.

"In their lairs, their chieftains spin new recipes for poisons and, some believe, sorceries. When their forces attacked Eveningstar, they had a weapon we didn't think anyone but us had: They could breathe fire."

Jennifer hugged herself with her wings. She was not crazy about spiders when they were an inch long and spun harmless webs in the front doorway. The thought of a spider her size that could launch into the sky like a rocket and breathe fire past poisoned fangs on the way down was plainly terrifying.

"What about Barbara's descendants?" Patrick asked.

To her own surprise, it was actually Jennifer who began to answer. "I've seen one," she whispered. She was loud enough that the others turned to look at her in surprise. "The dream . . . Ms. Graf. She was wearing shining armor and a crown. They use swords, right? She did. They speak Latin, I think . . . and I remember talk of justice, and laws, and prophecy. And death." She felt Catherine's wing claw reach out and grasp hers. Looking up at her grandfather, Jennifer shivered. "They're brutal."

"They are brutal," he answered sadly. "But I'm afraid even your potent imagination does not do them justice, Jennifer. While the werachnids act out of animal instinct, the beaststalkers—so we call them—act out of religious fervor. Barbara is their patron saint, and they seek us out in an effort to smite evil.

"Beaststalkers often have swords as you suggest, but they do not need them. They are masters of the duel, walking weapons that use light and sound to subdue even the most powerful of Allucina's other children. Their very voice can paralyze their foe. Some even—"

Suddenly Crawford stopped, as if something had occurred to him. He sighed and smiled apologetically. "I don't mean to scare all of you. Other than in dreams"— he looked meaningfully at Jennifer—"no weredragon has reported seeing a beaststalker for years. Be glad of that."

This did not completely reassure her. She looked into the lingering darkness under the sunlit trees nearby, half-expecting to see huge, bulbous eyes or the glint of a curved sword. But there was only the empty eagle nest.

"My grandmother says dragonflies are bringing strange news to her," Catherine offered. "She says we may see beaststalkers again, soon!"

Now Crawford actually chuckled. "Young Catherine, your grandmother is among the most revered of the elders. But I think Winona Brandfire's dragonflies may be a bit too anxious. We have not heard a whisper of any enemy since Eveningstar, and I doubt we will for some time."

Jennifer did not know much about weredragons. She knew next to nothing about their enemies, or how reliable dragonflies were as scouts. But she knew a thing about her grandfather. One of the things she knew was that when he wasn't being straight with her, he could never look her in the eye.

Right now, his silver eyes strayed across the lake.

* * *

"So, you wanna go turf-whomping?"

"Pardon?"

Catherine's eyes were full of mischief. "Turf-whomping! My grandma taught it to me. Tramplers do it a lot, since we can't fly for long distances."

Jennifer shrugged. "Sure, I guess."

"Follow me."

They left the cabin and went out to the southern pastures. There were still hundreds of sheep grazing—Jennifer supposed her grandfather bought herds and herds of them to support the refuge. While the fluffy white shapes scattered at their approach, Catherine paid no attention to them, but instead began running out onto the grass, parallel to the tree line.

"Just watch!" she called back over her wing.

Her bulky olive form rolled over the gentle, grassy slope. Flapping her tiny wings, she barely got off the ground. Instead of soaring higher, as Jennifer had learned to do, she let herself glide back down to the ground. Then, with a magnificent kick, she heaved into the air again. Another kick—*whomp*—and another—*whomp*. They were huge, slow-motion steps by the clumsiest lizard Jennifer had ever seen.

She chuckled to herself. It looked like bad flying, but it also looked like a ton of fun. Before she knew it she was off after her new friend, letting her wings cut through the autumn air and kicking at the pale grass with trembling legs.

"The dashers laugh at us when they see us do this, but frankly, I like being this close to the ground!" Catherine called out as Jennifer pulled up, so that they were *whomp-*

ing side by side. "It makes for easier acceleration, like a sprinter using quicker steps. Check this out."

She slammed her heels down harder and shortened her stride. And just like that she was leaping ahead of Jennifer. Then she suddenly veered sharply to the left, into the forest.

"You don't have to use the ground every time!" she called out behind her. "I tried this last time and crashed, 'cause I'm still new at this, but let me see . . ."

Jennifer turned to follow, her stomach fluttering—the trunks of the trees were fairly close together, and some of them had very low branches with heavy knots. She tilted her wings enough to slow down to a gentle glide with each *whomp*, so that she could watch.

But Catherine didn't get far. After maneuvering fairly gracefully through a cluster of oaks and kicking off a thick trunk so that she could accelerate, she found herself faced with some heavy, fragrant pines that were just too fat to avoid and too bushy to find purchase for another kick. She slammed into two pines at once, and with a squawk tumbled through the lower branches into a flurry of dead leaves.

"Catherine! You okay?" Jennifer couldn't stop giggling—it didn't look serious, by any definition. "I'm not sure that's how you're supposed to do it."

"Maybe I should watch my grandma a few more times," Catherine muttered, shaking the leaves and twigs from her wingtips. "Of course, she spends most of her time in Crescent Valley, and I don't get to go there yet."

"Do you think what the dragonflies told her is true?" Jennifer picked a string of moss off of her friend's scaly back. "I mean about enemies coming? Grandpa seemed skeptical."

"With all due respect to your grandfather, the Brand-fires's scouts don't make mistakes. It's our specialty, you might say. If they tell us something, it's happening. Something is on the way."

"But *what's* on the way? Beaststalkers?"

Catherine shrugged. "Or worse."

CHAPTER 9

Training

"Weredragons," Crawford announced, "do not exist."

There were five of them on the porch—Jennifer, her grandfather, Catherine Brandfire, Patrick Rosespan, and a creeper Jennifer hadn't seen before, with lavender scales and a shield of spikes protecting the back of his neck. They were the newest weredragons, and they were getting a short lesson from their host.

Patrick looked them all up and down after Crawford's remark. He grinned.

"No disrespect, sir, but I *feel* pretty real!"

Crawford took the snickers from the students in stride. "Thank you, Mr. Rosespan. You're as literal as your older brother, I see. I suppose I should be more exact. We are real, physically. And we have spiritual strengths that I will help you access in the weeks and months to come. But to the rest of the world, we do not exist. Or haven't you noticed?"

Patrick shifted uncomfortably. "I always kinda wondered why I never saw Eveningstar on the news after my
family escaped."

"My first morph was right alongside the highway two
months ago," offered Catherine. She frowned. "Sure, it
was nighttime, but nobody stopped to check on me. Not
even the state patrol."

"We hide here, but we probably don't even have to,"
Jennifer suddenly realized. "Nobody ever sees us flying,
or hunting, or anything, do they?"

"They do not have to," Crawford answered. "A beast
flying through the air like you, a beast suffering in a ditch
like Catherine, a whole town of beasts burning to death
like Eveningstar—these are all things that can be ignored
by the larger world. Eveningstar, after all, was populated
nearly entirely by weredragons. It was a rare refuge in a
world that would rather not notice us. Simply put, we are
not mundane enough."

"We're freaks," offered Catherine. The term startled
Jennifer. "But I always thought that would mean *more*
people notice me, not less."

"It depends, doesn't it? People typically react one of
two ways to something different. They ignore it if they
can, and they try to stop it if they can't. They only seek a
third way, to accept and adapt, if they have no choice.
And we're not so different ourselves when we're human,
are we? Before your first change, some of *you* may have
missed a thing or two you ought to have seen or heard."

As he spoke, the elder dragon's eyes settled on Jennifer. The meaning was clear—she felt a sudden pang of
guilt about her father and her remark yesterday about not
trusting him. Sure, he could have told her earlier about
weredragons. But couldn't she also have made more of an

effort to find out? How many times might he have tried to tell her, only to have her snap at him, or ignore him? Heck, she tuned out so many of his lectures, he could have given a slide presentation on weredragon anatomy in the kitchen and she probably would have missed it.

Crawford saw his message hit home and continued. "Our position is precarious. We're too strange to merit notice. Were we to force the issue, we're too few to defend against the inevitable backlash. The consequences would be horrible. Our refuges—this farm, others like it around the world, even Crescent Valley—are hidden, but they are not impregnable."

"This is depressing stuff," the creeper complained. "Why are you telling us this—to make us feel worse?"

"Not at all! But you need to know the truth. Many young dragons come to this change with a lot of anger, or resentment, or despair. They try to change what they are to get the world to accept them—or else, they try to change the world too fast, to make it again like it once was when people revered and respected us.

"Change comes to us all, and it will come to the world—slowly and steadily, like a tide that the moon pulls across an enormous beach. You cannot push the waves faster, and no one can build walls of sand thick enough to stop it. It comes when it comes."

"So we just sit here and wait for things to happen to us?" Jennifer asked. "That doesn't sound very productive."

"I wouldn't expect *you* to sit and wait for anything," Crawford said with a smile. "You will each have your role to explore in our community. You can see this in the way each clan supports the others. Tramplers are built for strength and ferocity, dashers for speed and grace, creepers for stealth and strategy. In our customs, our battles, even our hunts, each clan has a role to play. And within those clans, each individual finds his or her passion."

Jennifer thought about that. What did that mean for her? She didn't look or feel like she belonged to any of the three. Did she have a role in this community, or would she be cast out once everyone realized how different she was, and how badly she fit?

"Each of you will spend time this week with a more experienced dragon who can help you learn the skills specific to your type," Crawford continued. "Joseph will learn camouflage, Patrick will learn tail strikes, and Catherine will learn lizard-calling."

At this, Jennifer slouched, seething with resentment. "And what am I going to do? Learn nostril-picking with a wing claw?"

"You," he answered with narrowed eyes, "are going to learn all three."

"I'll bet my father put you up to that."

"Actually, Niffer, it was my idea." He closed in and bent over so that only she could hear him. "This isn't going to be a vacation, my dear. If you think your father was bad, wait until you hear *my* lectures!"

It wasn't so bad, she reflected as the week went on. Crawford gave lectures each morning and evening—stories and history about weredragons and their culture. During these times, she learned little infuriating factoids, such as the edict that she, like every weredragon, would have to go through fifty morphs—more than two years!—before they could even learn where Crescent Valley was, much less go there. Some sort of obnoxious test of maturity, she gathered from the rambling.

After several doses of this sort of thing, Jennifer decided learning new skills from the other tutors—*doing* stuff—was a bit more appealing.

She and Joseph needed to pick up the finer points of camouflage from none other than Mullery, the creeper who had emerged from the brush the day Jennifer had watched the hunt. He was a bit surly, and never let on if "Mullery" was his first or last name. Jennifer often had the impression he would rather be somewhere else.

The first lesson went passably well, given the dark cloud hanging over their tutor. When Joseph tried a tree-bark pattern, he was able to get appropriately rough-hewn lines. But Mullery ruled that the color was two shades too light, and the texture too spacious.

Jennifer herself could manage a lay-low camouflage that mimicked fallen leaves, but not much else. An attempt at tree bark ended up in a sort of rudimentary plaid, and her try at a rock, in Mullery's curt words, required "more mineral, less vegetable."

Tail-striking with Patrick, under the tutelage of his older brother, Alex, was a better spirit-raiser. Alex liked to speak in military shorthand (just like Eddie, Jennifer thought wistfully). According to the older Rosespan brother, dashers had strange oils throughout their bodies, allowing their nervous systems to act as generators. The prongs at the end of Jennifer's tail were longer than most dashers'—and of course, she was larger to begin with—so right away, results were spectacular.

"Wow!" exclaimed Alex, as a cascade of sparks blew apart an empty hornets' nest they were using for target practice. "Nice work! You acquired that target like an old pro. You'll be on dasher duty if we ever get you on a Crescent Valley hunt, and that's an order!"

That sounded agreeable enough, albeit vague, Jennifer decided later that week while lolling through woodlands with Catherine and Ned Brownfoot. It certainly seemed more exciting than Ned's first lizard-calling lesson.

Jennifer still wasn't sure what lizard-calling was, exactly, but to hear Ned tell it, it required near-perfect weather and ground moisture conditions. After putting off their first lesson for two days because "the moon war'nt right," Ned—who was at least as old as Grandpa Crawford—spent at least an hour looking for the right patch of ground to work on.

His kind, elderly, southern Missouri drawl made Jennifer impatient and tired all at once. "Young 'uns," he said as he paced, "never get th' hang . . . of summonin' crap . . . without th' proper beddin'."

"Here now . . . this otta work," he finally called out, right before Jennifer and Catherine gave up for the day. He was at the entrance to a low cave that was at least a quarter of the way around the lake, in a part of her grandfather's forest Jennifer had never been before. The leaves were scarce and the dirt less spongy. It reeked of dried dung left by indeterminate animals. "Now, girls, come on in . . . 'n' watch yer heads . . . It's *my* job . . . to find th' right spot . . . but it'll be *yer* job . . ."

"To die of the stench?" whispered Catherine.

". . . ta duck."

"Ow!" Catherine rubbed the back of her pale olive head where it had just scraped against a dip in the cavern's ceiling.

"Hey, Catherine," Jennifer asked when they had a moment alone. (This happened fairly quickly, as Ned felt— immediately upon their arrival at the cavern—that an even more choice spot of ground must lie deeper within, and so went exploring.) "Can I ask you a question?"

"Sure," Catherine said, grinning through vermilion eyes.

"You ever see, um, *weird* things when you're human?"

Catherine shrugged. "I daydream now and again. In Mr. Soule's history classes, I often drift and imagine myself flying or floating."

"Hmmm." Jennifer wasn't sure their experiences quite matched up. "Nothing about beaststalkers? Raining spiders? Sheep people? Vomiting up hearts?"

"Ugh. No." Catherine's reptilian face showed concern. "Have you talked to your grandfather about that?"

"Not yet. It's hard for me to separate what's normal for a dragon from what's not. I'm trying not to bother him with stuff that may not be important."

"Listen, Jennifer. If it's important to *you*, it's important. And you need to talk, believe me. I'm not that much older than you. Sometimes, fourteen years old seems like yesterday." Catherine sounded surprisingly sad. Jennifer was confused. Weren't the last couple of years in high school supposed to be the time of your life?

"I wish I had connected with my family more back then. I didn't realize until my first morph how much I really depend on them. When I was alone out by the highway, I was running away from home. They had told me about the whole weredragon deal, and I was freaking out. I didn't know whether to believe them or not. Either way, I was furious with them."

"Huh." Jennifer didn't know what to say. This sounded too familiar.

"Girls!" Ned's aged voice came trembling from deep

down in the cave. "Gimme a wing claw here . . . I think . . . I'm stuck . . ."

After freeing Ned's right hind claw from between two rocks, where it had slipped after contact with a patch of not-so-dry dung, the two of them convinced the elder dragon to get on with the lesson nearer to the cave entrance.

The trick to lizard-calling, according to Ned, was in the smoke you used to prep the ground.

"You gotta *pepper* th' dirt . . . like an omelet that ain't quite right . . . watch now . . ."

He snorted vapor from his nostrils and watched it float over the rocky floor of the cavern. Then, with a roar far louder than Jennifer thought this old man could manage, he punched the ground with a clenched claw.

An instant later, an enormous Gila monster came crawling out of the receding smoke. It twisted its massive head about, flicking its tongue, seeking its master. Once it found him, it curled up at his feet and stared at the astonished younger dragons.

"He's waitin' . . . for orders," Ned explained. The careful Missouri accent didn't sound so slow and dumb to Jennifer all of a sudden. "He'll stick 'round . . . up to 'n hour. Then you gotta . . . call new 'uns."

"We're going to do *that*?" Jennifer stared at the Gila monster. It looked large enough to swallow Phoebe with minimal effort.

"What did you think lizard-calling would be like?" snickered Catherine.

"Well, I dunno, but I didn't think we'd be . . . *calling lizards*. Cripes, that thing is huge!"

"You won't get 'un . . . like Trixie here. Not right

away. More likel'a mud turtle . . . or garden snake. Give
a try, Cat."

With furrowed brow bent low, Catherine puffed smoke
onto a patch of dung-lined pebbles. Jennifer peered in
closer to get a good look at whatever came out.

After a few seconds, Catherine roared—not as loudly
or well as Ned—and pounded the ground.

For a second nothing happened. The smoke dissipated.
Jennifer was just about to ask what Catherine did wrong,
when the pebbles suddenly began to shift, and out popped
a tiny black and yellow box turtle. Without hesitation, it
scurried to the cover of its mistress's left wing.

"Oh!" Catherine herself seemed surprised at the re-
sult. "He's so cute! I love box turtles. Oh, Ned, will I always get him?"

"Love at first sight," chortled Jennifer. Catherine stuck
out her forked tongue.

"There are ways t'get th' same 'un back." Ned nodded.
"Assumin' you don't get 'em killed."

"Killed?" Catherine gasped. "How would that happen?"

"We use them in war," Jennifer guessed.

Ned nodded again. Catherine's olive skin paled.

"But you can't . . . I won't . . ."

"Oh, Catherine, no one expects Boxy here to sail into
battle. But Gila monsters could, right Ned?"

"And snakes. Snakes're best for fightin'. They're fast.
Poisonous. Take stuff personal. Your turtle there, Cat . . .
heeza good-lookin' fella . . . prob'ly a family man . . . we
won't draft 'im just yet."

His easygoing smile calmed Catherine a bit, and Jennifer stepped up to take her turn.

She let the smoke flow from her nose and mouth. It
built up quickly and covered the ground around her wing

claws. She realized in a panic that her foreclaws were not anywhere as muscular as Catherine's or Ned's. *I'll have to make up for it in the vocals,* she told herself. Her tail twitched nervously.

A deep breath later, she let loose with the most ferocious roar she could manage. The noise blasted off the cavern walls and hurt her own ears. Ignoring the pain, she rolled up her tiny clawfingers and brought her fist down upon the cave floor.

To her utter astonishment and dismay, a pygmy owl fluttered out of the scattering smoke. With a panicked hoot and flurry of feathers, it scrambled up to her shoulder and buried its small but exceedingly sharp talons into her collarbone.

Jennifer tried not to wince in pain and embarrassment as she turned to Catherine, who looked ready to bust a gut laughing, and Ned, who seemed unimpressed.

"Okay, see, I have *no* idea where that came from. . . ."

The new moon came, and then another crescent quickly after that. About two and a half weeks would pass before the moon would shift again into its peculiar shape, and Jennifer into hers. As Thanksgiving approached, Jennifer found herself more and more accustomed to life on the farm, whether in the shape of dragon or girl.

Most of the dragons would leave the farm before they changed back to their human form. Surprisingly, one didn't leave—Joseph Skinner, the young creeper who took Mullery's camouflage lessons with Jennifer. Without much explanation, he set up in one of Grandpa Crawford's guest rooms, and his host did not argue at all, or ask questions.

"You'll find," he explained to her privately, "that every

once in a while, a young weredragon will show up with no roots. I've heard a bit about this boy's background, Niffer, and I'm not surprised he'll be staying with us. This isn't just a refuge for our kind during crescent moons, you know. It's a haven every day, of every week, for as long as I own this cabin. That's my duty."

Jennifer thought of Skip, and his moving to Winoka with his father after his mother died. "What's Joseph's story? Doesn't he have any family to go back to?"

"That's none of your business, or mine," he chastised. "It's enough that he wants to stay. There's room enough at the Thanksgiving table for all, no worries about that!"

That didn't satisfy Jennifer completely, but Thanksgiving reminded her of something else. "Catherine told me before she left that her grandmother's still hearing rumors from the dragonflies. Something's supposed to happen sometime after Thanksgiving. But you didn't seem to think much of her predictions a while ago."

Crawford slumped down onto a sitting room couch and rubbed at his fringe of white hair. "True, but I've heard a lot since. And I was more worried the first time than I let on, I suppose. Winona Brandfire's no fool, and she doesn't pass on news unless she thinks it's for real. What else have you heard?"

"Something plans to attack Crescent Valley. Something that doesn't belong."

He looked thoughtful. "And does that bother you?"

Jennifer shrugged. "I dunno. I don't even know what Crescent Valley *is*. And no one will tell me for fifty freaking morphs!"

"Forty-seven, now. Crescent Valley doesn't open itself up to just anyone, Niffer. You have to earn your way in. And there's no sense in telling you what it's about until you're ready to go there. The venerables wouldn't have it any other way."

"Okay, see, that's the sort of thing that drives me nuts about you. I ask about one thing, and you bring up something else I've never heard of. What's a venerable?"

He chuckled. "Sorry, Niffer. It's just going to take some time. In any case, those rumors sound like the same thing I'm hearing. Something plans to come, maybe to Crescent Valley and maybe not. Maybe it plans to come *here*. In any case, we've all got to keep our eyes open, in all phases of the moon."

"Beaststalkers?" she said breathily.

"Could be. Ned and some of the others, they've sent lizard scouts out around the ruins of Eveningstar, and other places. Something's gathering again. Hard to say who or what. Not friendly, though. Some of the elders think it may be looking for the Ancient Furnace again."

"The Ancient Furnace? But that was lost long ago—and it's just a story anyway. Why would anyone think it's here, or in Crescent Valley? Wouldn't we have found it by now if it was?"

"They don't care if we've found it or not. Wherever our enemies think it is, they'll go. A few elders also believe now that it was rumor of the Ancient Furnace years ago that attracted the werachnids to Eveningstar." He sighed. "How're your skills coming along?"

She welcomed the change of subject. "I can do tree bark and nest mix pretty well. And Alex says he's never seen a new dragon tailshock so well. I can flick a beetle off a leaf as I fly by!"

"Great! And how about lizard-calling?"

Jennifer's smile disappeared. "Oh. That's going all right. Catherine's been getting blue-tongued skinks pretty regular, now. And she even managed a hinge-back tortoise before she left."

"And you?"

She brushed her hair to one side and poked at the couch cushion. "Well, at least the owls stopped coming. But I can't get much more than a Jaragua, no matter how much smoke I make, or how hard I pound my fist."

"A jaguar?!?"

She sighed. "*Jaragua.* They're these lizards so small that they can fit on a quarter. I'm not surprised you haven't heard of them—only someone who sucks as much as I do can summon one."

"Don't be so hard on yourself, Niffer. Most dragons can't cross skills at all. *You've* got two and a half so far. Plus your fire-breathing is solid, your flying is second nature, and I've seen you turf-whomping and fishing. You're really catching on."

"I guess." She gave him a look. "You've watched me turf-whomp? What're you doing spying on me, anyway? Did Dad put you up to it?"

He diplomatically ignored the question. "You hear from your dad yet this week?"

"Not yet." Her father had called every couple of days to check in. The conversations were always brief, but friendly enough. What Catherine had told Jennifer about wanting to see her own parents made more sense as time went on. "I kinda miss him, and Mom."

"Hang in there. Thanksgiving's only a couple days away. They'll be proud of your progress. Maybe you'll decide go back home with them for a while."

"Maybe. I bet they'll drive me nuts in ten minutes."

* * *

It was actually more like three and a half, Jennifer mused Thanksgiving morning as she slumped in the cabin's dining room, back in dragon form. After hugs and kisses from both parents, and a satisfying slobber from Phoebe, her father asked how she was doing. When she made the colossal mistake of telling him, he wouldn't rest until he gave her an array of pointers on how to make better smoke, and pound harder, and a bunch of other stuff she felt was pointless since her father wasn't a trampler and had never summoned a lizard in his life.

True, the father who had left her on the cabin porch weeks ago had been uncharacteristically curt that day. But at least she had gotten in a word edgewise!

Elizabeth was more reserved than usual. Perhaps it was the presence of a virtual stranger the entire day—Joseph was polite to his hosts, though not much of a conversationalist. Or maybe it was because she was the only one not in dragon form. But it was plain to Jennifer that her mother had missed her. The older woman remarked occasionally about the crescent moon, and how it wouldn't wane enough for a few days for everyone to change back. Then she would look at Jennifer with obvious longing for her daughter's human face.

Thanksgiving night she lay in bed. The thought of changing back to her boring bipedal form raised mixed feelings. She both dreaded it and yearned for it, sort of the way she felt about carrying on with high school this year.

Then she remembered that for her, the change was even worse: School was probably over forever. What on earth would come next?

With that unanswered thought, she drifted off to sleep.

CHAPTER 10

Geddy

"Home at last!" she crooned, stepping dramatically through the front door to her own house back in Winoka. They had waited out the next crescent moon up at the farm, and it was a good week into December. So many things seemed so long ago. She almost felt newly born again—her human limbs weren't as weak or clumsy as they had been after her first morph, now over two months ago.

"Hey, where's the sullen teenager we've grown to love?" her mother teased softly.

"I've eaten her, because I'm starved. When's dinner?"

"As soon as your father can get it on the table."

Jonathan started for the kitchen. Jennifer went to the office computer to check emails. There were over a hundred for her.

They missed me! she thought with a warm glow, recognizing several of her school friends' addresses. She settled in for a comfortable hour of writing back.

It didn't take long for her good mood to evaporate. What on earth would she tell these guys? That she could summon an owl by slapping her wing on dirt? That skin camouflage was best mastered first thing in the morning, when she was freshest? They wanted details on her "hospital stay," but Jennifer had never been to a hospital as a patient—only to see her mother at work.

She discussed the problem with her mother, who looked thoughtful. "Tell them you're glad to be back, the food sucked, and the doctor was really cute but talks too much."

"Doesn't sound like a lot to say."

"Honey, that's all they want to know."

"Hmm. Maybe. But isn't this lying?"

Elizabeth kept an even expression. "You *are* glad to be back; you said it yourself. The food *does* suck at the hospital—I can vouch for that. And there's this cute new surgical intern there who likes to flirt over head traumas—"

"All right, all right, it's all true, just *please don't say anymore.*"

Returning to school the next day brought two bits of good news to Jennifer: First, the animal shapes were gone. There were no more Canada geese drifting through the school hallways, or horses galloping through the gymnasium. Her eyes let her see everyone as their normal self.

The second bit of good news was that her mother had been right: Vague statements were enough for her friends. Eddie and Skip had warm greetings for her, accepted her fumbling explanations without a blink, then instantly dived back into the complicated morasses of their own lives. They had missed Jennifer, but her peers were just as self-absorbed as she was. Probably just as well, she thought.

She wondered if she would have noticed that sort of thing before that first crescent moon.

Susan also seemed ready to be friends again. Jennifer knew this when Susan announced, "Okay, so, I'm ready to be friends again."

"Huh?" They were in study hall, ten minutes before the bell would ring and free them. Jennifer had been half-asleep, shading in sketches of the pigs and sheep she hoped she'd never see again. Suddenly, she came to full attention. "Hey, did you just say we're friends again?"

"Yeah, I guess. Just don't blow me off again . . . and try to stay off the drugs, okay?"

"Hilarious. Your future is in comedy."

"I mean it, Jenny. Just—keep it together, okay?"

Jennifer ignored the nickname. "You don't react well to change," she observed, not unkindly.

Susan wiped her eyes. "I just want things back to normal."

Jennifer looked at her friend sadly. Things had changed, and Susan's clinging to the past was only part of what bothered her. She realized with a start that in some ways she felt closer to Catherine, a high school junior who thrilled at every new lizard she called, than to Susan, who hadn't really changed since they were six.

Later, on the school's front steps, Skip bounded up to them with his usual alarming energy, flirted outrageously, and had her and Susan talked into a trip to the local fudge shop when Eddie wandered up.

"Fudge run, Eddie? C'mon, I'm buying. How 'bout a half pound of peanut butter marble chip marshmallow swirl?"

"Ugh, have another ingredient!" Susan spat.

"Well, he wasn't offering it to *you*," Eddie said. He turned back to Skip. "I'm ready for that mission!"

"Well, come on, ladies—you, too, Susan. If we don't get there quick, those rat bastards from the basketball team will have hogged it all."

"You just call them that because they lose, lose, lose. They need Jennifer on their team," Susan suggested. It was an obvious ploy at flattery, which Jennifer didn't mind at all.

They trooped down the steps, and Jennifer blushed when Skip threw his arm around her waist. Since he was flirting with Susan and tormenting Eddie at the same time, she decided it was just a friendly gesture and made no move to throw him off.

Besides, it was nice. And he smelled great.

A squeal of brakes interrupted her internal musing, and she looked up in time to see Eddie's father pull up beside the curb in the familiar brown pickup. He leaned over and bawled through the open window, "Ed! Shake a leg, boy. Training!"

They all stopped and stared at the stern face, which was redder and bulgier than ever. When Mr. Blacktooth caught sight of Jennifer, and then Skip's arm around her waist, his head quietly shifted from red to purple, and his cheeks looked like they might burst.

Uh-oh, Jennifer thought wryly, *I've tainted Skip.*

"Aw, geez, Dad, we were just gonna make for the—"

"Edward James Blacktooth! NOW!"

"Bye." With that sullen word, Eddie broke away from their little group, trotted to the car, and climbed in without looking back. As the car roared off, Skip spoke first. "Yeouch! Wonder what 'training' means?"

Susan sniffed. "Probably some anal-retentive lawn-mowing exercise. Mr. Blacktooth freaks out over everything. You know him, he's a total jerk. If my father acted like that, I'd ditch and go to my grandparents'."

"My father gets upset sometimes," Skip offered quietly. "But he knows not to push me too far. Not since Mom . . ."

Jennifer, who caught Skip's discomfort at the mention of family again, brought them back on track. "Come on, guys. The fudge won't come to us."

More subdued now, the three of them left the school grounds. Skip's arm slipped from Jennifer's waist. But before she could feel bad about that, she felt his fingers poke at her palm. She grasped his hand back.

The new kid had been there for her in Mr. Black-tooth's truck. And outside Mr. Pool's office. And drawing sketches in her room. And now, he was there for her more than anyone else was. Even Eddie. It made her happy, and also a little sad somehow.

"You should come over for dinner sometime with me and my dad." It was the next day. Jennifer and Skip were coming out of Ms. Graf's class after a deadening slide show on the anatomy of crabs, lobsters, and scorpions.

"Huh?"

"Dinner. You know. What you eat at night."

"Yeah, I know dinner. I mean, why?"

"Because if you wait long enough after lunch, you get hungry. You wanna come over tonight or what?" To Jennifer, he appeared nervous and annoyed.

"Is this, like, a date?"

"I dunno. I guess." Skip was sweating, his cocky expression replaced by something Jennifer had never seen before in him—fear. "You don't have to come to our house, if you don't want. We could all go out somewhere, like the food court at the mall."

"Your dad wants to meet me at the mall?" Part of Jennifer knew it was cruel to do this to Skip, but she had to admit she was enjoying it. She just had to be careful he wouldn't withdraw the offer completely—she *did* want to go.

"I've told him about you, and he wants to meet you. He's still a bit weird about me dating, since my mom . . . um . . ."

"Sure, I'll go." Jennifer was embarrassed at the mention of Skip's late mother. She hadn't meant to press him that far. "The mall sounds fine. I need to check with my parents when I get home. I'll call you tonight."

Both Mother and Father approved and, in fact, seemed relieved at her request.

"It's good to see you going out with friends again," Jonathan explained. "Do you want one of us to go with you? I wouldn't mind meeting this boy—"

"This is going to be stressful enough," Jennifer interrupted. "Another parent there would kill me."

"I'm just not sure you should do this alone—"

Fortunately, she had a backup plan already in place. "Susan's already agreed to go with me. Just drop us off at the mall entrance, and pick us up two hours later. No muss, no fuss. Okay?"

It worked out passably well, Jennifer thought later on after she had gotten back home. Susan and she were dutifully impressed by Skip's dad. He had the same greenish blue eyes and chocolate hair, he dressed in the casual clothes of a man who made his living in construction, and his eyes seemed always wrinkled at the corners in a friendly laugh.

"Mr. Wilson?!" He chuckled when Jennifer addressed him this way.

"My, what a polite young woman you are, Ms. Scales! Very well, Mr. Wilson will do."

Over take-out sushi, they discussed school, soccer, the upcoming Christmas holiday, and even a bit of Skip's mom. According to Skip and his father, she would take her son around the world—western Africa, Australia, and South America—as part of her studies in native cultures.

Suddenly, the conversation turned to Jennifer's own travels, and the one tense moment of the evening.

"Skip tells me you're away from school a lot, and that you're going through a tough time." His greenish blue eyes lost some of their sparkle. "I know something about what you're going through. I expect it isn't easy for your family."

She wasn't sure how to respond to this. Her blood was turning cold. What if Skip's mom, just like Susan's, had died after a long illness? She would never be able to explain to either of them the truth—not after faking the sort of sickness that had hurt them so deeply.

Seeing everyone stare at her made her realize she should answer. She chose her words carefully. "It's pretty hard. I'll be gone a lot this winter and spring. Skip and Susan have been very understanding. I'm lucky to have them as friends."

Susan reached out next to her and grabbed her hand. They exchanged soft smiles, but Jennifer felt even worse than she had before. She decided then and there: *I'll tell them both the truth. Soon.*

She just needed a bit more time to get used to the truth herself.

Weeks went by, and Jennifer supposed she was adjusting. Both her strange dreams and the animal visions were gone, and she supposed that had to count for something. She felt she could settle into school a bit, even though it still seemed pointless. The routine of classes and friends was still comforting, for however long it lasted.

Certainly her freakishness had its advantages, even in human form. One mid-December morning she jumped from the ground halfway up the icy trellis to her bedroom window without wings. And the school bullies certainly walked more softly around her. Word of her recurring sickness did not seem to overshadow word of Bob Jarkmand's pasting at her hands months ago. Skip called her "my bodacious bodyguard," which was as exasperating as it was endearing.

Christmas morning, she was in the shape of a girl, and even better, she was in the shape of a girl with an alarmingly high stack of presents. Both of her parents and Grandpa Crawford were there—Joseph insisted that he never celebrated the holiday, and would watch the farm for them while they were in Winoka—and they had all been very generous in this most trying of years.

She placed another sweater—this one a gorgeous riot of blue, gold, and green—on her new clothing pile, half-listening to a conversation between the other three. Most of her attention was on the next gift, the size of a shoebox with gold foil wrapping and bow, as her father filled her grandfather in on some development at work.

"—last week's city council meeting, where we were trying to get approval of a site plan—"

She shook the box. It rattled satisfactorily.

"—ran into Otto Saltin, of all people! I didn't even know he lived anywhere near here. He happened to have business before the council on the same night. Anyway, we steered clear of each other—"

She smelled it and grinned. The Godiva truffle box! And larger than ever this year, she noticed as she clawed the paper off in a single stroke.

"—company's been doing business in town for at least the last couple of years. I'll have to— Hey, not before breakfast, miss!"

"Aw, *Dad*," she whined. The golden box glittered invitingly. "Just one?"

"Just one would become just eight." Her father softened a bit. "After breakfast, go crazy. Have a truffle party."

"Thanks. And thanks for all the great gifts, you guys. It's—" . . . *been a tough year,* she thought. *Been great to have my space while I figure things out. Been even better to have us all together for the holidays. Going to be best of all to sneak a truffle out of the box when no one's looking.* "—er, it's really great."

"You're not done yet," Jonathan said. He rose and ambled upstairs. A minute later he came back down and handed her a small box with holes punched all over. It fit into her hand neatly. The logo for Daniel's Pets (the D was a curled up cat and the P was a dog sitting up on its hind legs) marked the sides, top, and bottom.

"What *is* it?" She gently tilted the box. Something skittered inside. "It's too small to be a puppy, unless you got me one of those irritating, yappy, small ones—"

"Ugh. No. I'd eat one of those before I'd have it in our house," he said with a shudder. "No, it's something more, ah, suitable to your nature. Some dragons like to have . . . well, they like to have companions."

Phoebe chose that moment to push her muzzle into Jennifer's lap. The dog got one whiff of the box, raised her enormous ears, and began to growl through her muzzle.

Jennifer flicked her on the snout. "Don't get jealous, Phoebe! It doesn't become you." The dog whimpered softly and jogged out of the room.

Lifting the top flap, Jennifer peered inside the box.

A small, delicate lizard gazed back up at her. It was a joyful, vivid green and sported a red streak down its back. Its eyes were tiny pools of fathomless black. The corners of its mouth were ticked upward in a permanent, silly grin.

"Huh! It's . . . um . . . it's . . ."

"It's a gecko. And let me tell you, that's no ordinary lizard. He practically leapt into my pocket while your mother and I were browsing the pet store. We had to convince the manager we weren't trying to shoplift him."

The gecko smoothly scurried up to the edge of the box, clung to the open flap, and licked its own eye with a lightning-fast, spoon-shaped tongue.

"He's adorable! What's his name?"

"You can decide that after you agree to handle his care or feeding. Or hers. Or whatever." Her mother's tone suggested not everyone had left the pet store happy.

"The cashier said it's a he," Jonathan offered enthusiastically.

"Yes, I'm sure it's a he! I just know it!"

Her mother smiled vaguely. "Fabulous. A telepathic

lizard. The next time you and he commune, make sure you both understand that neither your father nor I are responsible for him. There are some books in our room, and a tank, and supplies. You move it all to *your* room and set it up. Assuming you want to keep him."

"You bet! Oh, thanks, he's great, Geddy's just great! I can't wait to—"

"Geddy?" Her mother snickered. "Geddy the gecko?"

"You said I could name it, and that's the name I like," Jennifer said with a sniff. She didn't know why she had chosen that one. It just seemed to fit.

Geddy licked his other eye.

"Those books tell you all sorts of neat things," Jonathan offered. "For example, smaller geckos live for about fifteen or twenty years—the shop owner said he didn't know how old this one was, but figured he couldn't be more than a couple years. They shed their skin every six weeks or so in warmer weather and eat it. Also, if a predator catches one, it can detach its own tail! Also—"

"I'll read the books, Dad. Promise." She lifted Geddy off the box flap with a finger and held him up to her eyes. "I thought geckos made noise. Isn't that how they get their name—*gek-ko, gek-ko*?"

In response, Geddy licked one eye, then the other, then the first one again.

"He hasn't made a peep since we got him."

"Huh. I guess Geddy's a freak, just like me." But Jennifer said this with a smile. "Aren't youuu, my widdle Geddy-gecko-poo? We're two widdle peas in a pod!"

Phoebe whined from a distance. Elizabeth looked ready to retch. But Jonathan and Crawford smiled.

"I used to have a little fella just like that one," Crawford said. "You'll be surprised what a gecko can do for a dragon."

"Can it clean her room?" Elizabeth asked. She and her father-in-law exchanged looks, but Jennifer didn't notice. All she could do was titter as Geddy slunk across her hand and arm, up her ticklish neck, and through a mane of sliver and gold hair to perch upon her head.

CHAPTER 11

Newolves

They flew back under cover of darkness the day after Christmas, all three of them in a line—her grandfather, her father, and herself. She was looking forward to spending time as a dragon with her father—the bad feelings between them on that cold October morning had passed over time, and this last Christmas present had sealed the deal.

Said present was currently clinging to her horn with ferocious nonchalance. Jennifer had expressed worry that Geddy, being cold-blooded, would freeze to death, but the others had assured her he would be fine. Her mother agreed, with something approaching disdain, to bring up the tank and supplies in the minivan in a few days. In the meantime, the lizard would have the run of the cabin.

"We'll have to find you a cricket or two from the barn," she whispered to him as his spoon-shaped tongue hung out of his mouth a tiny bit. "Or maybe you'll brave one of Grandpa's hornet nests. They're a bit more sluggish in winter, you know."

Thick clouds hid the moon as they streamed through the night, a distance off the highway. The scent of snow was on the air at least ten minutes before the first soft flakes sprinkled their wings. By the time they reached the cabin, an inch of powder covered the driveway.

"I'd better go check in with the newolves," Grandpa called out as he veered over the eastern pastures. "Jon, you and Jennifer get set up, and let Joseph know we're back. Maybe he's got a bit of leftover mutton in the fridge? Don't eat it all! I could use a snack."

"Newolves?" Jennifer asked as her grandfather's dark shape disappeared quickly into the twilight. "I've heard that word before. What are they?"

"I doubt you'll see much of them," Jonathan told her. "Normally they stay in Crescent Valley. But your grandfather thought it would be a wise precaution to keep a few near the farm, given some of the rumors we're hearing. They're excellent guards, and fiercely loyal to our kind."

"Loving father. I can't help but notice that you haven't answered my question at all."

"Yes, well . . . just don't go out looking for them. They'll smell you well before you see them, and they're not easy to get to know."

Jennifer sighed as they landed on the northern porch. Joseph was waiting for them, and as luck had it, there was indeed leftover mutton, but not a lot of it.

"So what are we going to do tomorrow?" she asked her father as they hurried to finish off the meat before Crawford got back.

"Well, I don't suppose you want me looking over your

shoulder during your lessons. I'll probably just stay out
of your way during the day, and join you and your grandfather for breakfast and dinner."

"Do you think we could do a little ice fishing?" The
lake had frozen over well before Christmas this year.

"Sure." He laughed. "You'll see how nice it is not to
have to drill through the ice. Though plunging your head
into the icy water may get old after a few times. You
may wish you were spending more time with your tutors
instead!"

When she didn't smile at that, he leaned in close.
"Hey, I didn't mean anything by that. Grandpa tells me
you're absolutely amazing, at everything you do."

"Not everything." She pouted. "I still can't summon a
darned decent lizard."

"What, you're still worried about that? Don't fret,
sport. You'll be calling brontosaurs by Valentine's Day."

"They're called apatosaurs now, Dad."

"Dumbest name in the world. Makes 'em sound half as
big, with bunny shoes. Some things just shouldn't change."

Winter passed quickly by the lake, and friendships deep-
ened. Catherine, Patrick, and Joseph all made a point of
keeping meals with Jennifer, even when her grandfather
or father didn't join them for a story or history lesson. At
first this made Jennifer feel awkward since she was
younger than the other three, but as Catherine put it, "In
dragon years, we're all newborns."

She actually didn't see much of her father after the
first couple of weeks back—just an occasional drop-in
here and there, though he was always careful to call if
more than two or three days went by. He would often take

over a camouflage lesson for her and Joseph, sending their surly tutor off to disappear smoothly in the forest somewhere. In this formal setting, Jennifer found his lectures more tolerable. In fact, he seemed to make a point of keeping his words short and sweet.

As for her mother, beyond the briefest of stays on New Year's Eve (to drop off Geddy's tank and supplies), she barely came by. The cabin seemed to make the doctor uncomfortable, and Jennifer noticed that Crawford never asked his daughter-in-law to stay for long, even when there weren't other dragons about. When Jennifer asked him about this, he was rather terse.

"It's a matter for your mother and me," he told her. "Best leave it alone, Niffer."

So Jennifer spent most days during crescent moons playing sheep hunts with the other dragons, or creeping up on deer in camouflage, or zapping the pine cones off of pine trees with her tail as she whipped by. She kept up with her friends back home (mainly Susan and Skip) by phone, and did the occasional school project as time allowed. Her dragon friends followed a similar schedule, keeping up with their own studies as best they could while also helping Jennifer with her schoolwork so she wouldn't fall behind.

Joseph was the only one of the three she ever saw in human form. He was pale, of Norwegian lineage, with a blond crew cut and a quiet but easy smile. Because he was staying at Grandpa's cabin he naturally spent the most time with her. At seventeen he was an apprentice electrician, so he was able to help Jennifer with science and mathematics. Patrick was a history buff, and so during his crescent moon visits to the cabin, he would check her history and writing work.

Catherine was actually already taking a college-level

course in sociology and anthropology. Jennifer wasn't sure what this was, but she nodded politely when her friend pronounced it so seriously. She became a whole lot more interested when she found out what Catherine studied in her spare time.

"Newolves?" It was an early spring evening. Pale buds were forming on the tips of the deciduous trees, but the crescent moon was still visible through their stark branches. "You've seen them? What are they?"

The scales around Catherine's lips curled in a mysterious smile. "Now, you have to promise not to tell anyone about this. Grandma told me not to go poking around the forest, but I couldn't help myself. The past few weeks have been so fascinating! The potential advances in anthropological methodology alone are—"

"Yeah, yeah, yeah, that's great, *what are they?*"

"They're reverse werewolves," the older dragon explained. "Usually, they're just very intelligent, very large wolves. But every couple of days, they take human form. After I pestered Grandma for a bit, she told me they shift every fifty hours or so. But I want to do my own observations. So since early February, I've been slowly introducing myself to the dozen or so your grandfather has across the refuge."

"Wow, so you can talk to them now? Share meals with them? Play primitive games?"

"Um, not really. But when I fly overhead, they don't scatter anymore."

"That's quite the doctoral thesis you've got going there."

"Hey, it's progress. You wanna come along someday?"

"Thanks, no. If I want to chase animals around, I'll go after sheep. At least I can eat those."

Despite her skepticism, Jennifer found herself looking forward to Catherine's ongoing daily reports on the herd: what the youngest newolf cub had eaten, who appeared to be the alpha male, how a new mating pair was getting along. It became an elaborate secret that the two of them shared.

The spring mornings came earlier and grew warmer. During one late April sunset, when the latest crescent had almost finished waning in the sky and only one or two dragons were left at the farm, Jennifer decided to ask her friend if she could go along on a visit. Catherine's red eyes immediately lit up.

"Oh, yes, that would be great, Jennifer! The pack just settled into a new grove a bit west of where they had been before. I think it's a territorial push. They've acclimated to my regular visits, and I think they're ready for additional exposure to a monitoring agent. Just think of what we can learn about how they respond to observing our *own* unique social relationships!"

"Um, yeah, I guess. I just wanna see 'em. We'd better hurry, though—my dad's flying in later tonight before the crescent moon ends, and he'll get suspicious if I'm not around."

It had been raining all day and the early evening skies were still overcast. The oaks, walnuts, and maples now gave good cover to anything on the ground, and Catherine couldn't fly too well anyway, so it took some time for her to spot the right landmarks and lead them to where she was sure they would find the newolf pack.

"Here!" she finally called out from the ground, as Jennifer nervously skimmed the branches above and felt a few lingering raindrops flick her scales. "Come on down and look!"

Expecting to witness an exquisite gathering of primeval man-beasts, Jennifer cleared her throat, gently came down through the trees (being careful not to make any sudden moves), and gazed upon . . . a huge puddle of mud.

"What, is there a newolf taking a mud bath in there?"

"No, look! Right in the middle!"

Jennifer peered more closely at the puddle and saw, a bit left of center, an indistinct impression in the mud. Her father and grandfather had taught her a bit about tracks when they hunted deer, and this one looked strange. It might have been the print of a newolf. Or it might have been the print of a drunken timberwolf. *Or* it might have been a crater left by a small, bouncing stone . . .

"Um, Catherine . . ."

"They can't be too far! Come on, this way!"

Half-dragging her younger friend, Catherine pushed through the brush, making quite a racket and (Jennifer was certain) scaring anything outside of a cement bunker away. After a few moments, just as the last few rays of sunlight drifted through the wet leaves around them, she gave an incredibly loud hushing sound and pointed.

"Oh, Jennifer, look! Over there!"

Jennifer would never be able to put into words the sight that met her eyes as she followed her friend's finger. This was largely because she didn't see much.

"That was a fox, wasn't it?"

"No, no, no. *Behind* the fox."

"Oh for—Catherine, tell the truth. Have you actually ever *seen* a newolf?"

"Of course I have!" The older girl seemed hurt by the implication. "Plenty of times. I just think they're being shy around you."

"No, the *missing link* is shy. These guys are positively antisocial."

"It's getting late." Catherine sighed. "The crescent moon's only got a couple hours left in it. I'd like to get back home before then—it'd suck to morph halfway there and then have to walk in the rain."

"Okay. Well, thanks for the nature stroll."

With a sour glance, the trampler turned and lifted herself off the ground a bit, before whomping her way through the forest. Jennifer glided up above the trees and headed back for the cabin.

When she returned, Joseph was waiting on the porch for her. He had already morphed back, and had a suspicious look on his pale face.

"Where have you been?"

"Out in the forest."

"Doing what?"

Jennifer decided the truth would do. "Absolutely nothing. Since when is this any business of yours?"

"Your grandfather's out looking for you. He's worried. Your mom called."

"What did she say?"

"She says your dad left for here this morning. He should have been here hours ago."

Just then, the phone rang inside. Jennifer pushed Joseph aside, lumbered over to the phone, saw the incoming number, and knocked the receiver off with one claw as the other clumsily pressed the speakerphone button. "Mom?"

Her mother's voice was very faint.

"Your dad's in trouble, honey."

"Mom, what's going on?"

"Come home, sweetheart. Please. Right now."

CHAPTER 12

Investigation

Elizabeth Georges-Scales had never looked so old to her daughter. Tears clouded her green eyes, and her shoulders slumped over the kitchen table. In her quivering hands was a single scrap of paper, which had been crumpled and smoothed multiple times.

She didn't look at Grandpa Crawford or Jennifer as they entered in human form. Handing her father-in-law the note, the woman barely moved her mouth and did not make eye contact.

"Someone slipped this under the door early this evening, after I called the first time. I didn't hear or see a car in the driveway."

Crawford looked at the scrap, read what was on it, and walked out immediately. His anger was obvious. Elizabeth did not even try to make him stay.

"I'd say we have until the new moon's over before

your grandfather goes out and does something rash," she explained as the door slammed.

"What, three days away?" Jennifer was aghast. "What do we do until then? And why is he so angry?"

Elizabeth held up the paper so that her daughter could read the single word scrawled there:

Prophecy.

Jennifer felt a numbness slide down her spine. The sounds and sights of her dream with Ms. Graf filled her mind. *Justice. Law. Prophecy. You die, worm.* She leaned against the table and sat down quickly.

A few moments passed. Jennifer took a gulp.

"So he's dead, then. That's what beaststalkers do, right? Kill dragons?"

Elizabeth crumpled the note again. "We don't know it was a beaststalker, honey. And we certainly don't know that he's dead. He may have been taken alive."

"Where?"

Her mother just shrugged.

"Who was the last person to see him? Where on the road did it happen? What do the police say?"

"Good heavens, Jennifer, we can't involve the police. They wouldn't take this seriously. We'll have to do this ourselves."

"What about Grandpa? Shouldn't he help?"

"I think your grandfather would rather be alone. He'll send word to the elders. By the time the waxing crescent comes, they'll know what they want to do next."

"But I don't just want to sit here and do nothing!" It was almost a scream. Elizabeth looked up at her calmly, but Jennifer could see her fingertips trembling.

"We will not do nothing. We will think through this.

Together. Then tomorrow, we'll be better prepared to take in whatever evidence we find on our own."

Geddy nestled on Jennifer's shoulder, and Phoebe (with a wary eye toward the lizard) nuzzled Elizabeth's belly.

"We start with what we know," Elizabeth began. "Your father left just before noon. It takes about two hours for him to fly up to the cabin. An ambush would have to be reasonably certain of the path Jonathan was taking, and the closer one got to the cabin, the more certain the path would be. We'll search the road close to the cabin first, and move slowly southward."

"This could take days!"

"It will take however long it takes. In any case, we can be pretty sure the note tells us your father didn't meet with an accident. For someone to have taken him, and link him to some prophecy, they would have to know what he is and where the farm is. That suggests a certain amount of preparation."

"Okay, so they were after *him*. Why? I mean no one in the human world would be after him, would they? What about the military? For experiments?" She shuddered. If the military wanted him for some strange research project . . ."

"It's not the military," Elizabeth assured her. "First, they don't go around leaving notes on doors. Second, your father and friends have contacts there. Please recall your grandfather served in the U.S. Navy Special Forces, in his youth."

"All right, so it's gotta be beaststalkers, or werachnids."

"Or other weredragons," her mother reminded her. "Good and evil are not always so clear-cut, dear. I'm sure there are werachnids who disagree with each other, or beaststalkers as well. After all, have you always gotten along with your father?"

Jennifer returned the wry smile. "I only ever got angry at him for those interminable lectures. And missing my soccer games."

"Silly girl. He never missed a single one."

Jennifer felt the color drain from her face. "Never? Wha . . . what about his business trips?"

"Haven't you figured this out yet? There were no business trips—at least none that he'd take when you had a game. He was always on the edge of the school grounds, camouflaged of course, within sight of the soccer field, watching you. Every minute. Of every game." The tone was gentle, but the words hit Jennifer like bricks. How had she not realized this before?

"He saw the championship game?" How she had torn into him for that, behind his back! She was not sure she could stop the tears she felt building.

"Nothing could have kept him away from that."

Jennifer couldn't speak. She had been so completely wrong about so many things. And it was possible she would never be able to make it right. "He always *said* he thought I was a great soccer player. But I never believed him, because I didn't think he ever saw me play."

Elizabeth's hand ran through Jennifer's hair. "He'll see you again, sweetheart."

"Yeah." Jennifer blew her nose. "I guess. You really think we'll find him?"

"I know that nothing will stop the Scales girls, if we work together."

She smiled. "That's pretty good, Mom. You actually sound sure of yourself."

Her mother didn't return the smile. She grabbed Jennifer's chin and stared into gray eyes with determined green ones. "Nothing will stop us, if we work together."

They continued talking for a little while longer. It turned out that Elizabeth knew a great deal about dragons and their world, which didn't surprise Jennifer, since the woman had been married to one for years. Given the prominence of the Scales family, it made sense that Jonathan would be a target. He was not an elder—Crawford had that title for their family—but had the respect of weredragons. Because of his status, Elizabeth guessed, Jonathan would be in an excellent position to hear of an upcoming attack.

"So an invasion is coming?" Jennifer deduced after hearing her mother lay out these details. "Of Crescent Valley? And they took Dad because he heard about it?"

"That is one possibility. There are others. For example, your father is a weredragon in his prime. He would be suitable for study, if his captors wished to know more about how . . . about weredragons." Elizabeth tried to sound clinical, but her voice broke toward the end.

Jennifer shivered. She thought about *Grayheart's Anatomy,* that beautifully illustrated book in her grandfather's library. It was hard not to imagine the gorgeous images of skin peeled back, bones cracked, and organs revealed. They didn't seem so gorgeous anymore.

"Also," her mother went on quickly, "some enemies are aware of weredragons' capabilities. They may see creepers, and your father in particular, as possible spies. They may assume dragons are planning their own attack. In that case, they would want to question your father about what *he* knows about *them.*"

Jennifer studied her fingernails for a while. "Mom, even if they wanted to study weredragons, it would be more useful to keep one alive. At least for a while. Right?"

Elizabeth shuffled down the couch and held her tightly. When the phone rang, they were both tempted to ignore it, but Jennifer had to answer.

It was Joseph, calling from the farm. "Your grandfather just got back. He told me about the note. Is there anything I can do?"

"Thanks, Joseph. I don't think so. Listen, I'm a bit worried about Grandpa. Maybe you could just . . . be with him?"

"Of course." She heard the young man's voice break on the other end of the line. "I'm so grateful to him, and to Jonathan, for taking me in. If you need anything, let me know."

"Thanks again. Good-bye."

No sooner did she hang up than her mother was up and off the couch.

"Listen, honey." Elizabeth's voice brooked no argument. "Sitting here dwelling on this is not going to help you. And we're not going to get any magic phone calls. There's nothing we can do during nighttime—at least not until you're in dragon shape—and it may be a while before you can go out with friends again. Maybe you'd like to go out tonight? With your friends?"

"But that's dangerous! And you'd be here home alone!"

"I didn't say you wouldn't have a chaperone! We both need to get out of this house."

It was a hard night, but not because of any chaperone interference. In fact, Jennifer was amazed at how well her mother blended in with the mall scenery, several yards behind her and her friends.

Rather, it was difficult because Eddie wouldn't come. He had been Jennifer's first phone call.

"Um, I don't think so," he had said in a distracted voice, before she could even finish the invitation.

"Eddie, I'm sorry I'm not around so much anymore. But Susan and I mended fences, and—"

"That's not it. Not really, anyway. I guess things are just . . . changing."

And then he had hung up.

"He's a twit," Skip explained to her later as she and Susan eyed designer shoes in the mall's department store. "He's been like that to us lately, too. Hasn't he, Susan?"

"Ever since about a week ago," Susan agreed, obligingly bulging her eyes as Jennifer showed her the price tag on a pair of "discount" loafers. "His dad drives him to school and picks him up, so we can't go anywhere together. Not that he even sounds sorry about it. He just mumbles stuff about how there's extra work for him around the house, that kind of garbage."

"I've never seen a kid so enslaved by a parent," Skip added. "I mean, my dad tells me to do stuff I don't want to, and my mom was always a bit strict, but . . ." He coughed a bit, and reached into his windbreaker. "Speaking of which, I know I haven't said much about Mom. She was part Sioux, and she took me all around the world while she studied native cultures—western Africa, Australia, South America. Anyway, she gave me this a couple years ago. I figured it would look nice on you."

He pulled out a rawhide necklace with a wooden circle hanging off the front. Carved into the disc was the image of a large elm leaf.

"It's the Moon of Falling Leaves," he explained as he

reached around her neck to put it on. "It represents October. And November, too, sort of. Um, anyway, since we met in October, I thought—"

Jennifer kissed him squarely on the lips.

"Whoa there, tiger!" He backed up and tried to look calm, but the red flooding through his cheeks betrayed him. His eyes darted to Jennifer's mother, but fortunately she was studying some purses a couple aisles away. "Er, you're welcome. You must be going through a tough time at the clinic, and well, if there's anything I can . . . well . . . er . . ."

"Excuse me, third person here!" Susan called out with a look of disgust. "Are we going to the ice-cream store, or fudge store, or what?"

"I have all the sweets I need," Skip leered, regaining composure. Susan rolled her eyes as Jennifer chuckled.

Then Jennifer remembered her father again and felt worse than ever that she forgot about him for even a moment.

Two hours before daylight, she and her mother were on the road to Grandpa Crawford's cabin. Jennifer insisted on bringing both Phoebe and Geddy for comfort, but most of the car ride was spent admonishing one pet to stop provoking the other.

As it turned out, there was no trouble finding the site of the struggle at all. Less than a mile from where the driveway meandered away from the highway, there was a high dirt shoulder for about twenty yards, and nearby a small grove of trees. There were fresh tire tracks on the muddy shoulder, visible even from a distance. Elizabeth pulled over.

"Keep the pets in the van," she told Jennifer. "I don't want them messing with any tracks that are down there." So while the two of them carefully studied the shoulder and nearby ditch, Phoebe and Geddy glared at each other from opposite ends of the van's interior.

"Down here," her mother called out after just a few moments. The fresh spring wind was not strong enough to sway the damp field grass down in the ditch, and it was immediately clear what she was pointing at.

"Someone was lying down here." Elizabeth then nodded at a larger indentation in the grass just south of it. "And this is where your father landed."

"Maybe he saw someone lying in the ditch, and stopped to see if they needed help," Jennifer guessed. "It looks like there was some rolling back and forth."

"That would make sense. But there's still something strange. Your father's been on edge for the last few weeks, and I think he'd be cautious about someone lying on the ground, whether they looked hurt or not. It's unlikely whoever it was could surprise him from that position."

Jennifer looked at the grove of trees nearby. One tall oak bent over the ditch where they stood, and its heavy branches swayed in the breeze. A small bird nest was nestled in the lower branches, but she heard no song.

"Hang on a sec, Mom." Effortlessly, she leapt up the tree trunk and onto the thickest branch that overhung the ambush site. The nest had small bluish eggs in it, even though no parent seemed to be around.

"Sparrows," she called down. "They ought to be dive-bombing me, like they do when Phoebe or I poke around that nest outside our garage. But something's spooked them away, for good I'll bet." Perched over her mother, she looked straight down into the older woman's eyes. "If

I knew you were going to be standing there, this would be a great place to jump on top of you."

Elizabeth nodded. "So there were at least two."

Jennifer didn't respond. She was staring at the brush just twenty yards away, behind her mother. Something was in the bushes, watching them.

It was a wolf, but more than that. The size of a small bear, and the color of warm sunset, its bulk was nearly invisible behind the cluster of birches. Two ashen eyes looked back and forth at the two humans with a mixture of judgment and desperation. Immediately, Jennifer knew two things: First, that she was looking at a newolf; and second, that this was only a chance meeting. This creature did not know any more than she did about what had happened here—it only knew something had come close to its territory, and was here to investigate. Just like them.

The eyes stopped darting and settled on this strange girl, high up on the branch. Jennifer could feel its gaze pierce her human skin and examine the shape it saw inside. *It recognized her.*

Perched precariously on a tree branch, with soft pale skin and fluttering gold and silver hair, under broad daylight with no sign of a crescent moon, Jennifer had never felt more like a dragon. A piece of her world stood before her, quiet and accessible. She ached to reach out and touch it, even though it was far below. As she lifted her hand, it opened its mouth and seemed nearly ready to speak, if that were even possible . . .

"Honey, what are you looking at?" Elizabeth's clarion voice disturbed the quiet connection. "What's back there?"

In an instant, the newolf's face was gone. With a start,

Jennifer caught a glimpse of its furry flanks and, she thought, a smaller shape clinging to its backside—a pup.

A strong desire to leap off the branch and chase it seized her. She wanted to try to communicate with it, touch its offspring, see if either of them knew anything. But she knew it would be useless, and she let out a long breath.

"Nothing, Mom," she called back down carefully. "Just a deer, I think."

She examined the branch, as well as the next two higher up but she found no further clues. Some of the bark seemed a bit thin in places, but that could have been anything.

Neither she nor her mother found anything like blood around the scene—just indentations, shoe prints leading in and out of the ditch, and a swath of grass that may have been smoothed down by a heavy, dragged bundle.

"So this is what we know," Elizabeth summed up as they got back into the car. A distant howl pricked Jennifer's ears, but her mother didn't seem to hear it over the engine. "There are at least two ambushers. They know what your father is and they know about your grandfather's farm. One of them is fast enough to knock a dragon unconscious—yet apparently did not want to kill him."

"Werachnids?" Jennifer asked, shaking thoughts of the newolf away. "Grandpa says their chieftains can work sorcery. Maybe one cast a spell on Dad, to knock him out."

"It's possible. The crescent moon was nearly over, and I gather different individuals morph at different intervals. One or both of them could have been able to drive a truck. But usually, the simplest answer is the right one—I think something more regularly human in shape did this. Certainly the note points us that way."

"Beaststalkers, then. They wrote 'prophecy' in the note. What prophecy do you think they're talking about?"

Elizabeth shook her head sadly. "It's hard to say," she sad with a sigh. "Both your father and grandfather put some significance into the fact that your scouts had heard rumors of war, and of the Ancient Furnace. If beaststalkers have located your grandfather's farm but are afraid to approach it, it would make sense to kidnap your father, learn all they could, and set an invasion plan based on what he tells them."

"So they'd learn about Joseph and the bees."

"And other things, from what I hear. Your grandfather is very clever, and not all of the defenses will be obvious. How much anyone learns from your father depends on how . . . forceful . . . they are."

Suddenly, Jennifer didn't want to talk about this anymore. "So what do you think Grandpa and the other dragons will do, when the crescent moon comes?"

This made her mother quiet for a while. Her knuckles turned a bit white around the steering wheel. Finally, she said, "Honestly, Jennifer, I have no idea. You have a better idea as to how your grandfather thinks than I do, at this point. What do *you* think?"

Jennifer stared out the passenger window as the Minnesota farmlands swept by. "When I was younger, I only thought of Grandpa as a grandfather, like most kids would. He would tell great stories, and go fishing with me, and all that. But this past year . . . I've seen a new side to him. Something heated, impatient. Like how he treats you."

This earned a strange look. "You've noticed?"

"It would be hard not to. He wanted his son to marry another weredragon, didn't he? Not you."

The next words came out very carefully, even for her mother. "Jennifer, your grandfather loves you deeply and unconditionally. But he's quite traditional. Enemies have driven weredragons from one place to another for some time, and he has lived to see many friends and loved ones suffer. There are not many weredragon families left.

"For as long as I've known him, I've tried to respect his heritage. While your father and I were engaged and your grandmother was alive, I would try to find meaningful trinkets and books related to dragons for their birthday, and Christmas presents. But this just made things worse."

"Is that why you order him those ugly horse blankets from Iceland every year, now?"

Elizabeth grinned. "The horse blankets avoid conflict. He does love his horses. I think he's actually beginning to look forward to my blankets, now. Maybe it's wishful thinking."

"You do that a lot," Jennifer observed.

"Do what a lot? Wishful thinking?"

"No, not that. You avoid conflict."

"Hmmph."

They rode in silence for a few minutes, and then she added: "I'm a doctor, honey. I heal. I see the results of conflict every day—school bullies who provoke my daughter, family members who hurt each other, and complete strangers who go at each other's throats because they're just a tiny bit different. No, I am not a big fan of conflict. I prefer discussion, and open minds."

"That sounds nice, Mom. But someone who disagrees with you has taken Dad."

Elizabeth did not answer.

CHAPTER 13

The End of the Trail

When they got home, there was an unwelcome surprise waiting for them. Scratched into the green paint of their front door was a single word:

Furnace.

Jennifer lost it. She began kicking at the scratch marks furiously.

"Come out!" She screamed to the air above her. *"Come out and fight! Cowards!"* She punctuated each sentence with another kick. The door rattled on its hinges.

"Ssshhh!" Elizabeth pulled her back away from the door in a hug until her daughter collapsed. "Baby, that's not going to help! That's not going to get him back."

Jennifer could only sit on the doorstep in her mother's arms, sobbing. Her mother cried with her for a while, but before long the wheels were turning again. "Whoever did this left evidence. Let's get to work. You look around the house, and I'll focus on the doorstep. Come on, baby, get up. That's it. Can you do this?"

With a sniff and a nod, Jennifer got started. Unfortunately, Phoebe had been out of the car for a few minutes, and the few places where there might have been visible tracks were her favorite places to run. Before Jennifer could begin to interpret the few undisturbed impressions she could find, she looked up and saw a face looking out the window next door.

It was Mrs. Blacktooth, glowering at her.

Suddenly, a lot of things made sense. The hatred this family had for her. The way their church had rejected her mother years ago. The word "prophecy." The way they would watch her father, and all of the Scales family, closely. How easy it would be to slip next door that morning and scratch the front door while no one was watching. And above all, the way Eddie had been acting lately.

"Hey!" she called out to the woman in the window. In an instant, the scowling face disappeared. *"Hey!"* She began to walk across the yard toward the Blacktooth house.

"What's going on? Jennifer, where are you going?"

"It's *them!*"

"Honey, what do you—no, wait!"

Elizabeth tried to grab her daughter by the shoulder, but her hand was too easy to shake off. It took a bear hug in the middle of the lawn to get Jennifer to stop her march and pay attention.

"Mom, it's *obvious!* They're trying to get the furnace and they took Dad because they think he can help! Look at the evidence!"

"Jennifer, come inside. Let's talk about this—"

"He's been gone more than a day. If he's over there—"

"You can't know that. And if he is, what are you going to do about it?"

"I don't need to be in dragon form to kick those jerks' asses." She started to move again, but Elizabeth held on with both arms clasped.

"Not every problem can be solved by kicking a jerk's ass, sweetheart. And we don't even know it's them. You're jumping to conclusions."

"What's your plan, Mom?" Jennifer shouted, redirecting her rage. "Sit at the kitchen table and work through all the possibilities while Dad dies next door? Are you really that unfeeling?"

Her mother's eyes narrowed. "Get over yourself, kid. You're way out of line. I deal with death every day. And I'm telling you that if you go through that family's front door, you'll die."

Jennifer stopped struggling and stared. "You know what they are, don't you? You've known, this whole time. We've been putzing around the highway, and *you knew!*"

"We still can't be sure it's them, Jennifer. We have to approach this methodically, based on evidence and a plan. That's why police usually handle—"

"Oh, no, of course, Mom! It's probably not *these* beaststalkers. It's probably the beaststalkers two doors down! Or the ones at the bakery, or the bookstore! I can't believe I've wasted this day with you. Dad could have been home by now." With that, she broke free from her mother and continued toward the Blacktooth house.

"Jennifer, don't!" She could hear her mother about to cry again from the edge of their lawn.

"I can't believe you're such a damn coward! We're talking about *Dad!*"

Her mother's voice was desperate now. "Jennifer, if you go in there they'll kill you. They must know by now what you are. Please. Come back into the house. I can help. We can do this together, if we talk it through."

"You go ahead and talk, Mom. Talk all you like." She was at the front door. It stood stark and black before her. Without looking back, she raised her foot and kicked it off its hinges.

Mrs. Blacktooth was waiting for her in the foyer. She was a tall woman, though not as tall as Eddie or Jennifer. Her raven hair streamed down her shoulders onto a housewife's modest blue-and-white-checkered dress and frilly apron. Meticulous makeup shaped her nose and cheeks, and her sapphire eyes flashed with disdain. Across her carefully manicured hands, she held a long sword. The blade did not shine—instead, it seemed to suck the light out of the doorway.

"We have learned what you are, worm."

"Where's my father?"

"We know what he is, too, now. You cannot save him."

"Want to bet?"

Jennifer took a step forward. In a flash, the tip of the dark sword pointed at her throat.

"The Blacktooth blade has killed a beast in every generation, for the last two thousand years. It will kill again today." Something moved behind Mrs. Blacktooth.

"Eddie!" she called out. It was indeed Eddie, but not as Jennifer remembered him. His face seemed older, drawn. "Eddie, please!"

"You should leave now," he told her over his mother's shoulder. "Your father isn't here."

"Where is he?"

He ignored the question. "I can't save you."

This betrayal was too much. For what seemed like the hundredth time in the last day, she felt tears well up. "Eddie, how could you?"

"That's enough. Justice must be served. It's time to die." Mrs. Blacktooth stepped forward and pulled her sword back to strike. Jennifer flinched.

Then the sword came down—but slowly, and by its wielder's side.

"You are lucky today, worm. Your mother is here. By my people's code, I cannot kill a child before the eyes of her parent."

"My mother wouldn't care if you did." The words sounded wrong to Jennifer as she said them, but she could not help herself. Too much was happening to her, all at once.

"Do not let me find you alone. Ever."

"Go to hell." Jennifer backed away, still wiping her cheeks. Neither Blacktooth moved until she was out in the road. She backed away from her waiting mother.

The idea of going back home was humiliating. And there was no point staying here, if Eddie was telling the truth. But where could she go?

She felt Geddy's feet on her shoe. He swirled up her leg like a tree trunk, crossed her stomach, and settled on her left shoulder. With a turn of his tiny head, he opened his bright red mouth and hissed at the gaping front doorway of the Blacktooth house.

"Jennifer!" Elizabeth's called out desperately.

She didn't even turn to look. A mixture of anger, shame, and fear drove her in the other direction. The Blacktooths had marked her father for a freak. Now he was gone, her mother was useless, and she was alone.

It was several miles to the mall, walking the same

route she had the October night she had first morphed. Whether it was that memory, or just the rage and frustration that seeped out of her very skin, Jennifer thought she felt her insides swirl a bit. It was nothing, of course—the next crescent moon was still days away. Easy to shake off, the feeling was soon gone. By the time she got to Winoka's typical mall, with its typical parking lot and typical crowd of people and cars, it was midafternoon.

It was unseasonably warm. She felt the heat and her own pain, but very little else. She was thirsty. If she went to the ice-cream shop, she could order a malt and think about what to do next. Maybe she should try to call Joseph or her grandfather up at the farm . . .

"Jennifer!" The most welcome voice in the world.

"Skip!" She practically tackled him with her embrace.

The delight in his face turned to worry as he saw her desperation. "What's the matter?"

Jennifer finally reached the point where she couldn't hold back any longer. On the spot, without pausing or thinking, she simply poured out her entire story, from the fateful night in Mr. Blacktooth's truck to her father's disappearance to the scene at Eddie's house. She didn't know how he would take it, but the more she told him, the better she felt, and the more right it seemed to share.

When she was finally done, he stood there with wide-open eyes for a minute or so.

"Skip? Hello?"

"I'm with you." He gulped and tried a game smile. "This is pretty heavy stuff, Jennifer. Maybe your mom's right—maybe you should go home and talk this through."

"Haven't you been listening?" She could tell from the way he flinched that he wished he hadn't been. "She doesn't want to do anything, or confront anybody! She's blathering on about talking, and waiting, and all this time the Blacktooths have my dad socked away somewhere!"

"Eddie says they don't have him at their house?"

"Yeah. He might be lying, of course. But I don't think so. They didn't seem scared of me at all, so they would have just told me if they had him in the basement."

"Huh." Skip thought for a moment.

"What?"

"Well." He paused. "Remember that night back in October you first changed, when Mr. Blacktooth was asking about my dad?"

"I guess. There was a lot going on."

"Well later that night, he called about some work around town my dad was doing. Dad talked to him for a while and gave him some information on an undeveloped property at the edge of town. We never figured out why he was interested. A few weeks later, Dad said that Mr. Blacktooth bought it."

"So?"

"Well, there's no one around for miles," he explained slowly. "Nobody's built anything on it, or near it. And during the winter, Eddie and I went down there a few times for snowball fights. There's a huge entrance to the town sewer system right there. If I wanted to hide something, or someone . . ."

"Skip, you're a genius! Come on!" She left her malt half finished on the table and pulled him out of his seat. They had only gone a few steps when they ran into Susan.

"Hey, guys! What's up?"

Ten minutes later, as Jennifer finished telling her everything she had told Skip—it felt so good again!—Susan looked as though she wished she had never asked.

"Wow." This was all she said for a while.

"Susan, I'm so sorry I told you I was sick. You, too, Skip. But we have to find my father. Will you please help? Three is better than two. Mr. Blacktooth may not be alone, and Dad may not be in any condition to—"

"Jennifer, hold on!" Susan stopped cold.

She turned impatiently, guessing what her friend was going to say. "What?"

"Listen, I'm just a little freaked out, and that's okay, I believe you. And I forgive you for . . . for pretending you were sick, like my mom. But we can't just go running into a sewer to face this . . . whatever you call it."

"Beaststalker."

"Yeah. I mean, it sounds way too scary, for me. Jennifer, I'm sure you don't want to hear this, but I don't think I can go with you."

Instead of getting angry, Jennifer took a deep breath. "Susan, I've given you a lot to take in. I can see you're really worried about doing this. That's cool."

Susan exhaled.

"So you go home. Please . . . just don't tell anyone about this." After a quick hug, she and Skip left their astonished friend behind.

Winoka's southeast side was primarily an industrial park. A few family farms pressed up against a strip of dingy wetlands that separated them from the park. It was to this strip, and alongside a steep hill, that Skip led her to the sewer entrance.

The culvert was large enough that they could nearly stand straight up inside. Before they went in, Skip clutched her arm. He was visibly shaking.

"Jennifer. This is for real. You could get hurt. Are you sure you want to do this?"

Jennifer turned her face up to the sky. Two eagles were circling far above. The scent of lilacs was thick in the air. "All I can think about is my father, and how much he loved flying." She looked back at Skip. "You're a great friend, Skip, but I have to set that aside if you're not with me. I'm doing this for my dad. This is no time for cold feet."

"Right." He didn't look happy at the thought, but her resolve was apparently contagious. "Let's go, then."

The culvert led deep into the hillside and they faced their first problem—the darkness. Fortunately, Skip had a solution.

"Dad smokes cigars," he explained as he flicked a lighter. "He's always looking for a light."

It flickered faintly, but it let them see an opening directly in front of their feet that they might have fallen into otherwise. Ladder rungs were built into the concrete, all the way down into blackness.

"I'll go first," Skip offered.

"Very chivalrous. But remember Bob Jarkmand?"

"Hmm. Yeah, okay, I should stop coddling you."

Smiling back at him, she took the lighter and carefully stepped onto the first rung. A few steps down, she tried to get a look around—but she could barely see past Geddy, who sat calmly on her shoulder, much less anything about the sewer around them.

The smell, however, was unavoidable.

A year ago, the darkness and the stench would have been too much for her. She knew she would have gone running back to her mother (or her father, had he been available). But today, she would endure it. She had to.

That thought carried her all the way down to the last rung and onto a new level of the sewer system. Now she could hear running water. There appeared to be a narrow stream going through this hall, or room—maybe a utility room? The lighter did not reveal much.

Then, on the wall in front of her, she saw the third one-word message from her father's kidnapper, written in the substance it identified:

Blood.

The rashness of her pursuit finally hit home. *They were expecting her.* She looked back up at Skip to tell him to hurry back up. He seemed almost frozen on the rungs above her, staring at her—or behind her?

Before she could decide, the shadow behind her swung. The blow landed on the back of her neck, and with an *oomph* she crumpled to the floor. Her last sight was of Geddy scrambling into the safety of a dark corner as the lighter went out and she slipped into nothingness.

CHAPTER 14

The Ancient Hearth Relit

When Jennifer woke up, she found herself in a window-less room with rocky walls and a dirt floor. The only light came from beyond a single door of metal bars. A weight lay upon her shoulders. When she reached up, she felt an iron collar and chain around her neck. It was loose, but she still couldn't lift it over her chin. Using her fingers, she followed it back to its bolts in the stone wall.

Waving the faint odor of sewage away from her nose, she caught movement close by. She backed up quickly and called out, "Who is that? What do you want?"

"Jennifer, you're awake!" It was her father's voice.

In a dimly lit corner, Jonathan Scales was slouched on the floor. A rumpled wool blanket was next to him on the floor. He wore a chain like hers and looked as though he hadn't had much more than water. His unshaven face was gaunt and his gray eyes were sad. "Jennifer, why did you come? There's no way this was your mother's idea!"

She tried to go to him, but the chain held her back. In her rage and sorrow, the best she could manage was to touch his fingertips with her own. "I'm sorry, Dad, I came here to save you. Skip was with me. Have you seen him?"

"Honey, Skip . . ."

Jennifer felt a lump in her throat. "What happened to him? Where is he?"

"He's around," interrupted a familiar voice outside their cell. The tone was friendly and a bit patronizing. Jennifer strained to make out the shape beyond the bars.

The tall man had long fingers wrapped around the bars. While his face was in shadow, Jennifer could make out long features and dark hair. He worked keys into the lock, and the door swung in.

As he stepped inside their cell, he flipped a switch, and a naked bulb high above their heads cast a stark light. Jennifer could see him a lot better now.

Her heart sank. "Mr. Wilson?"

He gave her a gentle, fatherly smile, as if he were meeting her for coffee. "Actually, you made an incorrect assumption when you met me for dinner last December. Skip uses his mother's last name. Mine is Saltin—Otto Saltin."

Her heart was still dropping. She had heard this name used, in hushed tones by her father, around Christmas.

Before she could put any more pieces together, another figure slouched into the room. Now her heart hit rock bottom, as her cheeks flushed in confusion and anger.

"You!" The chain snapped taut as she tried to surge forward. She gurgled curses with enough venom to make Skip sidle back a step. The boy would not look up.

Otto Saltin chuckled gently. "She's a real spitfire, Jonathan. No pun intended! If I had a daughter like that, I might be more careful about whom she hung out with."

"If I had known that you and Dianna Wilson had a son," Jonathan croaked, "I would have been more careful about Jennifer's friends."

Skip sniffed the air miserably. "Dad, do you have to keep them down here? This place is rank."

"Sorry, son." Otto actually seemed to mean it. "I told you from the start, this wasn't going to be easy for either of us. If you've developed feelings for Jennifer, you'll need to set them aside now."

"I've . . . developed . . . a feeling!" Jennifer grunted as she clutched at the iron collar. Her eyes bulged and she felt the blood rise in her ears. "Come closer . . . and I'll . . . express it!" Below the collar, she felt the Moon of Falling Leaves medallion that Skip had given her. She ripped it off of her throat and flung it at him. It smacked the wall by his head and clattered to the floor.

Suddenly, she felt a familiar twinge in her spine. She panicked as she wondered how long she had been down here—had she been asleep two full days? Would this change help her, or hurt her? And just how tight would this iron collar get?

There was no time to reflect. With a hiss, she weathered the surprise of hardening scales, unfolding wings, and an erupting nose horn. It happened faster than ever before. Otto Saltin's expression barely had time to change from wonder to triumph before she was fully morphed.

"You see, Skip?" He sounded as though he was explaining a football game to his son. "She's the enemy. She lied to you, but we knew it all along. No time for doubts, son. We're moments away from winning it all."

"She actually told me the truth. Just before we got here." Skip glanced up, but didn't dare give her more than a quick look. He seemed both embarrassed to have tricked her, and terrified of what she had just become.

Jennifer growled at them both. The collar was less loose around her neck but still fit. She supposed this was why they used this on her and her father, instead of handcuffs, or . . .

She stopped cold and looked over at her father.

He was still in human form. *He hasn't morphed.* His expression was difficult, somewhere between astonishment, awe . . . and pride?

This made no sense. Jennifer looked to her enemies, and back to her father, and then back to her enemies.

"It's interesting, isn't it?" Otto seemed completely unsurprised by what had happened. The friendly wrinkles around his eyes tightened. "You have to wonder—is the problem with you, or your dad?"

She thought for a moment, then bowed her head. "It's me, isn't it? Always me. I'm the freak."

"Right. *You're* the aberration. The crescent moon's still thirty-six hours away, but here you are with your pretty scales and wings. Can you explain it?"

Jennifer did not answer. She looked again at Skip. The traitor was staring right at her now, swallowing hard. What was going on?

"Perhaps you know about the infatuation most dragons have with the number fifty," Otto began to explain pleasantly. "Fifty seeds in this or that ceremonial drink, stories of Allucina and her fifty children, and so on. No doubt, your hidden Crescent Valley refuge has fifty written all over it—"

"You'll never find Crescent Valley," she promised

through gritted teeth. "I have no idea where it is anyway, so if you're going to torture me, go ahead and get it over with. Even if I knew, if you think you could make me betray my friends . . . my *real* friends . . ." She spat this last out at Skip, who looked back down at the floor.

"Please don't interrupt." Otto's voice turned stern. "You don't have to tell me a thing. In fact, if I could find a muzzle big enough, I'd use it on you." Then the affable tone returned. "You see, Jennifer, I don't need to know where Crescent Valley is."

"You do if you want to find the Ancient Furnace!"

His eyes lit up. "So you know about my plan? Clever girl. You sure do know how to pick 'em, Skip . . . although of course, a *good* father helps his kid find the *right* friends." Otto shot Jonathan a look, but the chained man did not return it. Jennifer sensed surrender and failure in her father's limp head and shoulders.

"No doubt you've figured that much out because some tortoise or baby alligator was snooping around on your behalf," their captor continued. "Or maybe your elders finally caught on after Eveningstar burned to the ground. Kind of silly of them, if you think about it, not to see the whole truth."

The mention of small lizards made Jennifer think of Geddy. She looked around the cell as subtly as she could, but could not find a trace of her pet.

"I see whole truth just fine. So does my family. You just want to find the Furnace so you can have more power. Because you're weak!"

Suddenly, Jennifer remembered—more power, like breathing fire. *Fire-breathing.* Why hadn't she thought of this before? She opened her mouth to unleash an inferno—

Otto waved his long fingers. "Numb."

Before she could release the fire, Jennifer collapsed in a scaled heap on the floor. Her eyes rolled back, and she felt drool slide out the corner of her mouth.

He stepped forward, pulled out a handkerchief, and gently wiped the corners of her mouth. Jennifer tried to open her jaws and bite him, but she could not even do that much. "I do want more power," he agreed, "but I am not weak. You cannot withstand my powers. Don't you know what stands before you?"

Jennifer's words were slurred. She could barely move her tongue, much less her lips. "Beeeasststaaalkerrr . . ."

Otto actually laughed. The jolly sound echoed off the cell's walls. "Beaststalker! Did you hear that, Skip? See what these overgrown lizards are afraid of? Centuries and centuries after Bruce and Brigida and Barbara fought, after Eveningstar and everything, they're worried about beaststalkers. They haven't really learned yet."

Now he snarled viciously. "I'm not a beaststalker, dragon-girl." Whipping out a syringe, he bent down and jabbed her in the wing. She barely felt the prick. He drew out some blood, and then turned the needle toward himself and plunged it into his arm, emptying the syringe and muttering in a strange language.

Where's a raging case of encephalitis when you need one, she yearned silently.

"And now, to break the chains of the crescent moon," Otto announced with a step back.

The morph took Jennifer by surprise. The first thing to change was the man's head—it got longer, as his body below the neck got shorter and fatter. His jaws opened wide, split all the way back to his ears, and swallowed them. Mandibles sprouted out of the resulting hole.

His skin went an inky, shiny black and thick hairs

grew—black in the front, red and yellow on his abdomen. With a sickening splitting sound, his two arms broke into four, and so did his legs. He crouched down on the eight appendages.

Finally, the eyes emerged. The two originals blackened and bulged to the size of dinner plates. An additional eye burst out on either side of the main set. And finally, like sentries around the sides and back of the head, four more evenly spaced swells appeared.

If Jennifer hadn't been struck down by sorcery, she would have screamed. As it was, she managed a gasp and a mild squirm backward from the man-sized spider.

Otto's knife-sized mandibles clicked with every word. The odd, fatherly voice was still there. "Now you can see the face of the enemy you *should* fear, dragon-girl. With the help of your blood, I can take my form at will, independent of the moon's cycles. But that's not all this blood can do for us. Your capture will be the end of your race. I suppose I should thank you. You'll be so important to me, to Skip, to all of us."

His gratitude infuriated Jennifer. She began to feel past the numbness—the sorcery was wearing off, and she could speak with some effort. "You'll never get the Ancient Furnace!"

The mandibles vibrated in what could only have been a gentle laugh. "You still don't get it. None of your kind did. That's why no one protected you.

"*Find* the Ancient Furnace? *Get* the Ancient Furnace? I *have* the Ancient Furnace, Jennifer Scales. I have *you*."

It may have been the sorcery reasserting itself, but Jennifer went numb again. "What?"

"As I was trying to tell you before you rudely interrupted me the first time, you dragons have an infatuation with the number fifty. It isn't completely unfounded. If dragons spent less time hunting sheep and more time searching into the past, like I have, they would no doubt have learned the full prophecy of the Ancient Furnace. Every fifty generations, the blood of all dragon clans combines within a unifying figure. This blood *is* the Ancient Furnace. The one with the Ancient Furnace roiling through her veins wields incredible powers, and strengthens all who surround her. Or him."

Prophecy. Furnace. Blood. Jennifer recalled the messages that Otto and his son left for her.

"Powers like fire-breathing," Jonathan Scales guessed from where he lay. Jennifer could see that his concerned eyes had returned to her. She felt miserable, stupid, and used. Her father had not been the target. He had been the bait. And Skip had lured her right into the trap.

"Indeed," Otto agreed. "Breathing fire is a skill we have sought for a long time. Six years ago at Eveningstar, suspecting Jennifer's powers and how you might use them against us someday, we tried to find and kill her. As a chieftain among our kind, I could work enough sorcery to arm our troops with fire for a short while. The effort nearly destroyed me. After that, I decided I was going about it wrong. Instead of knocking myself out to kill her, I decided to lure her in and use her.

"I needed to be patient, since her blood would do me no good until she had her first morph. Fortunately, Skip and I moved into town just in time.

"Our first plan was to invite her over for dinner and just take her there, alone. But Skip began to think he was on an actual date, it seems, and so moved the location from our house to the mall." The hiss the massive spider directed at Skip betrayed a fury that had not entirely passed since last November.

"You didn't tell me what you had planned until after then!" Skip protested. He pointed at the syringe lying on the floor. "And you never said anything about blood, or hurting her!"

"In any case," the arachnid continued, "it would not have been advisable, to attempt to kidnap a young woman in front of several hundred witnesses. So the opportunity passed. Soon after that, you were gone for extended periods, in all phases of the moon. So I had to set up a slightly more provocative trap. I didn't mind. Spiders love traps, you see.

"And the trap worked. Anytime I need it, the power of the Ancient Furnace will be a mere injection away. Not just fire-breathing—I'm interested to see what beasts I can call to my service, or how easy it will be to hide in plain sight. How delightful your daughter's so talented. And a shame, I suppose, that she'll never get to use those talents again."

"What the hell do you mean by that?" Jennifer saw the outrage on her father's face—and the alarm on Skip's. How much had Otto really told Skip before getting him to lure Jennifer into the sewer?

"Don't panic, Jonathan. If you'd been listening, you'd know I have no intention of killing her." Otto was clearly enjoying this, rubbing his four forelegs together. "The boost her blood gives me is temporary. I need a continual supply."

"You come near my daughter with that syringe again, and she'll cram it up your bulbous ass," Jonathan promised.

The beast's posture betrayed a loss of good humor. "I don't doubt it. That's why I'll have to poison her into a permanent coma. I'll take what I need, when I need it. She'll never feel a thing. And she'll never see you die for what you did to our family."

Skip's thin voice rose. "Wait a sec. A coma? Forever? And you'll kill this guy? Why, because of Mom? Dad, you didn't . . . this is—"

"SILENCE!" The enormous spider shuffled its legs with lightning speed to face its human son. "I told you she would survive without pain. That's all you needed to know, son." The voice through the mandibles softened. "I don't expect you to understand anything else, Skip. Not until your first change."

Jennifer remained silent. Conflict between bad guys was good. Plus, she was pretty sure the sorcery was almost completely spent. She twitched her tail and curled her wing claws. Otto either didn't see this or didn't care. He kept his focus on his stubborn son.

"Dad, whatever this guy did, it's not worth murder!"

"He's right," Jonathan chimed in. Jennifer silently congratulated her father on not sounding at all desperate. "You can't expect to leave no trail behind. Both my daughter and I will be missed. And I imagine if my daughter knew where to find you, my wife will, too. You can expect authorities here at any moment."

The thought encouraged Jennifer. Her dad was right—maybe Susan had gone for help, too!

"You're quite a ways away from where Skip led your daughter," Otto informed them, "in a section of the sewer system virtually no one knows about but my own construction company. No one followed you here. No one will look for you here. You'll die here, Jonathan Scales, and your daughter will live out her days in this cell. Sleeping comfortably." He finished with a soft gurgle.

"*I* know where they are," Skip said steadily. To his credit, he stared all eight of his father's eyes down. "And I know this isn't what Mom would have wanted."

"You're a child," Otto sneered. "What do you know about what your mother wanted?"

"I know she didn't want *you*."

Otto's left foreleg jabbed up and pinned Skip to the wall. He did not sound fatherly at all anymore. "You ungrateful twit. You'll stay silent. And you'll come to appreciate what I've done for our family, and all our kind. You'll watch our destiny unfold, and you'll show respect."

With that, he let his dazed son go and spat on the ground. A puddle of venom sizzled upon the cement floor. He brought his right foreleg down, and dipped the claw in the venom until it shone with a light green coating.

"Now stay still, Jennifer, or this will do worse than knock you unconscious." Otto's spider shape positioned itself so that he looked directly at Jennifer.

As she stared back into the front four eyes, she found herself mesmerized with fear. She thought back to the butterfly that had put her into a trance, that day in Ms. Graf's science class. From there, her life did not flash before her eyes as much as unravel backward . . . the soccer championship . . . seventh grade, then sixth . . . elementary school graduation . . . the burning of Eveningstar . . .

Before her mind could go any further, Otto rushed forward and brought his foreleg down.

"NO!" With equal speed, Skip pushed off the cell wall and leapt forward. The distraction was all Jennifer needed—she scrambled back, and Skip rushed into her place.

With a cry, Otto altered his strike to avoid poisoning

his son, but the stroke was already nearly complete, and the claw grazed Skip's chest.

Nobody moved. They all watched Skip grab at his chest, feel the bubbling wound, and open his mouth. Then he staggered back into Jennifer and collapsed.

Otto saw this and was quick to anger.

But Jennifer was angrier, and quicker.

A blast of flame streamed across the room and engulfed the spider. He squealed like a monstrous pig, and forgetting about his own son's safety, he opened his mandibles and breathed his own salvo of fire.

She didn't have to think at all—it came as instinct to protect the unconscious boy in her arms. Her wings wrapped around Skip, and she turned her head down so that the heat bounced harmlessly off her armored back and wings.

"Fire may not hurt you, vermin, when you're in dragon form . . . but your father won't be so lucky . . ."

Letting Skip fall to the ground, Jennifer moved toward her father to protect him—but she had forgotten about the collar and wall chain! There was nothing she could do as Otto reared back to prepare a new volley of fire. With a cry of frustration, she sought her father's eyes one last time. But he was not looking back at her.

He was looking at something scuttling beneath the arachnid's spindly legs.

Jennifer squinted at it. It was Geddy.

Had Geddy followed them? If so, what—?

Before she could piece it all together, something moved into the doorway behind Otto and an intense light flooded the room. She shut her eyes against the pain it caused. Jennifer heard Otto scream, and then another sound filled her ears. It was a battle cry—deep, horrible, and petrifying. She slammed her wing claws to her ear-holes and began screaming herself.

A tiny corner of her mind recalled something Grandpa Crawford had said: *Walking weapons, using light and sound . . . their very voice can paralyze their foes . . .*

A beaststalker! Eddie had snuck away from his parents to help after all!

The light and the noise persisted. Even with eyes and ears closed, the assault on her senses was devastating. "Eddie, please stop that!" She couldn't even hear her own words.

The noise stopped. The light dimmed a bit beyond her eyelids. She dared to open them and gaped at what she saw.

The beaststalker was larger than life. Jennifer knew that the Blacktooths were tall, but seen from the floor of a cement cell in a sewer, this one was a tower. A full helm with no visor—how could he see? she wondered—glowed with a pure light. A drawn sword fed off the helm's light.

The rough leather armor may once have been white, but was browned with dirt and blood and time. Over this was a cape of black, thick, flowing fabric.

"Hurry!" The voice was high and clear, even through the helm. "I wounded him, but he will be back."

Jennifer finally noticed that Otto was no longer in the room. The dark sword swung through the air, making her flinch—but it cut the wall chain, not her, and with a loud *chink* she was free.

Another stroke and Jonathan was also free. He struggled to get to his legs. The beaststalker helped him up and supported him as they left the room.

"Wait a sec, Eddie!" Jennifer looked over at Skip. He

was lying faceup, shirt torn and chest wound still simmering with venom. "We can't leave him here. He'll die, or worse."

The reply was impatient. "If you want him, carry him." And with that, the beaststalker dragged her father out of the room. Geddy bolted after them.

CHAPTER 15

The Beaststalker

It was lucky for Skip, Jennifer decided as she rolled him onto the wool blanket her father had used in the cell, that she was a forgiving soul. His wound looked nasty and they were his best hope for quick medical help. Her wing claw cramped as she dragged Skip out of the room by pulling on the corner of the cloth, but somehow she managed to stumble out and follow the others.

Otto's lair was different from a typical sewer. For one, there were lightbulbs hanging every few yards throughout the network of rough-hewn tunnels. Second, the dimensions of the hallways were large—at least ten feet from side to side, and floor to ceiling. Third, there were other cells. Some were empty, and some housed unseen things that skittered and hissed in an unfriendly fashion.

Now was not the time for investigation, Jennifer decided. She kept her horned head down and her hind claws moving. They went on for at least a mile, slightly uphill, with Geddy slipping around the feet of those in front. Jennifer became more and more grateful to the gecko—they passed through several intersections, and took at least three different turns. Without the tiny lizard's memory and sense of direction, she realized, they would never have been found.

Skip became heavier and heavier as she dragged him on the blanket. "Eddie, how much farther?" she called out.

"The main junction is up ahead. After that, a few hundred yards to the ladder shaft."

"Okay, I can walk now." Her father's breath sounded ragged but stronger, and Jennifer began to feel they might actually make it out.

Until they heard the sounds of hundreds of clicking mandibles in the darkness ahead.

"He's summoned help," Jonathan guessed. "Except I'll bet it's not *lizards* he's calling."

"Dragon!" The voice through the helmet had a power that compelled her forward. "Drop the traitor! You should be up here with me!"

"I'll take Skip," her father volunteered. Jennifer let her burden slide to the ground and stepped up to the front of the group. Geddy quickly ran up her hind leg and found a comfortable perch on her back between her wings.

She winced as that awful noise and light began to fill the room. "No, Eddie! Let me take care of this."

The clicking got closer and closer. Up ahead and a few yards around a corner, the last of the ceiling bulbs cast a shaky light on a widening of the hall and a large opening where a barricade of boards and stones had recently been knocked down. Beyond this opening was wide-open darkness—the sewer junction Eddie had mentioned, Jennifer guessed. There was movement on the floor, but it was difficult to tell what it was, or how many.

"Now! Breathe your fire!"

"All right already!" she hissed back. Clearing her throat, she opened her jaws and let loose with the largest inferno she could muster. The flames flooded the cement floor and broke through the barricade opening, where it roasted about a dozen brown recluse spiders the size of lobsters. Their legs seized and curled, their eyes popped out, and their burnt bodies rolled onto their backs.

As the heat and light retreated, Jennifer made out the shadows of at least a hundred more recluses scrambling to take their place.

"Did it work?" Jonathan shouted out from behind them.

"Um, kind of . . ."

"Keep the fire going!" A swirl of black cape and a smoldering sword leapt forward to meet the onslaught.

"But I don't want to burn . . ."

"Breathe!" urged her father. "Beaststalkers can withstand your fire. Working together is our only chance!"

"Fine, if you insist," she shrugged. As her partner brought down the sword's point into the cement floor, she let loose with another sheet of flame.

This washed past the beaststalker's ankles and over the crack where the sword tip pierced the floor. Suddenly, the flames took on a bluish hue and accelerated forward. The new wave of spiders coming into the hall had no chance to react—the blue nova blasted through and carried their ashes back on top of those behind them. For a moment, the clicking echoes subsided, as if those left were uncertain what to do about this combined threat.

Unfortunately, they did not hesitate for long. Jennifer

could see them collect themselves and surge forward once again. Otto's new army seemed endless.

"If he got *my* powers," she complained out loud, "then *why* doesn't *his* summoning suck as much as *mine?!*"

"Jennifer!" Jonathan was standing at the corner, looking back down the hallway they had used. His voice had a twinge of panic in it. "They're behind us!"

"Hold the front, Eddie!" Jennifer wheeled around and raced back down the passageway toward her father and Skip. It was true—Otto must have left a small army of recluses behind to close ranks and overwhelm his enemies. They covered the hallway floor, walls, and ceiling only fifty yards distant. As their legs and bodies ran over the lightbulbs, they cast frightening shadows forward.

"You'll need to summon help," Jonathan told her.

"I can't!" she pleaded. "Every time my wing claw comes down, another pathetic lizard the size of a coin comes out! I've never called anything capable of stopping *that!*"

"Think of something!" He smiled at her desperately. "You can't give up now, ace. We need you."

Their rescuer's voice shared her father's desperation. "They are multiplying! Even with sound and light, I cannot hold them all back for long!"

An idea struck Jennifer. She hissed vapor onto the floor, pushing it as far toward the oncoming spiders as she could. Then she spread her wings, which grazed the wall on either side, and gently sailed toward the new enemies.

Then, as she flew, she kicked the ground with her right *hind* leg as hard as she could.

Although she nearly hit her head on the ceiling from the rebound, she didn't have to look behind her to know that something had risen up—something large—through the summoning smoke.

"That's it, Jennifer! Keep going!"

She was only a few yards from the spiders now. Greeting them with a volley of flame carefully mixed with smoke, she sailed into their midst with another *whomp* on the ground. Again, something sprouted—but she didn't have time to look back and see.

Her next breath sprayed the walls and ceiling, as well as the floor. She looked ahead for an end to the army, but did not see one. Turning back seemed like a good idea now.

She folded her wings and planted a foot down amid the smoke of her last breath. Now she could see her product. A spray of legless bodies had exploded out of the point of impact—black mambas, at least twenty of them. The brownish-gray snakes were twice their natural size and entered the fray immediately, lashing out at any foes that survived Jennifer's fire.

Wait until Catherine hears about this! She couldn't help but grin. She should have known when she first noticed her smaller wing claw that she'd have to do things differently from a normal trampler dragon.

As she looked back down the hall where she had already stomped twice, she saw dozens of other mambas spread out in battle. They were larger and faster than the spiders. They reared up with their black jaws open wide, struck to sever the recluse's head and legs from its abdomen, then slithered down the hall in search of more targets.

"Jennifer!" Jonathan's voice echoed down the hall. "We need you back here!"

Even though the corner was far away, she could easily make out a flash of brilliant light and heard a short beaststalker shout. It hurt, but it wasn't enough to stun her. Trusting her new army to guard this front, she glided over them and rejoined the others.

Otto had been busy in the junction room. Despite the eight-legged bodies strewn all over the hallway entrance, it seemed that there were more alive than ever. Beast-stalker tactics were failing—Jennifer guessed that they were better at mighty duels with singular beasts than holding off swarms of mindless intruders.

"Get down!" Jennifer ordered. She sped through the air behind a stream of smoke and fire. Her father ducked just in time to avoid getting burnt and clobbered. In the space between him and the retreating beaststalker, Jennifer slammed both hind legs into the smoke-covered floor. She felt snakes lift off in her wake as she vaulted over the beaststalker and landed on the other side, pounding the ground with both feet again.

Eighty-odd new serpentine soldiers slithered by her side and went right into battle.

There were even larger spiders now—none nearly as huge as Otto had been, but certainly sergeants in the field. They were gray wolf spiders with black stripes, and unlike the recluses, they leapt instead of crawled.

Jennifer focused her attention on these as they popped out of the junction room. She swung around and zapped each with her tail as they entered the hall, knocking their fiery corpses back into the junction room. One or two of them were caught in midair, mandibles poised to strike. The snakes shattered the ranks of smaller spiders, and soon the others were able to join and help her. The beast-stalker's sword swirled through the air, bolstering the serpent line where it weakened and grappling with those wolf spiders that kept away from Jennifer.

With Jonathan shouting the all-clear in back, and seeing the resistance collapse before them, Jennifer finally surged into the junction room.

It was a shallow dome, perhaps thirty yards in diameter and ten yards high. A paved stream of rainwater cut the floor in half from left to right, and another stream came from directly in front of them to form a T in the center of the room.

There was a large pillar of stone jutting out of the water at the joint of the T. A ceiling shaft above it led high above, letting a tiny bit of daylight through. Other than that, the chamber was dingy and dark. The construction felt different from Otto's hidden lair; it was probably built by the town decades ago.

The mambas slithered over the floor and over the streams, mopping up the last few spiders. Before long, all they could see or hear was dripping and rushing water. But they could not truly see the far side of the room, and this worried Jennifer.

"Do you think he stayed behind to fight?" she panted.

"I don't know," Jonathan grunted as he lay Skip down for a moment. "He may have felt the army he left behind was enough."

"It almost was. Eddie, do you see anything?"

"Stop calling me Eddie," the voice behind the helm snapped. "No, I don't see him. But that means nothing."

Jennifer realized the voice sounded like a young *woman's*—not a young man's. How stupid of her! She should have noticed from the start.

"Susan?!"

The beaststalker turned, but then a couple of things happened at once.

First, a blazing salvo erupted from the top of the

stone pillar. Streaks of fire coursed through the entire chamber, roasting the snakes they hit and lighting up the surprise on Jennifer's face. She heard her father shout in pain behind her.

At the same time, the top of the pillar bent a bit, so that it arched over the surprised beaststalker. A spindly, hairy leg whipped out and struck its target in a shower of sparks. The warrior crumbled to the ground.

"Susan!"

Jennifer launched into the air and straight at the top of the pillar. It was obvious who was there, hidden behind an aged-brick camoflauge pattern. Another talent he had inherited from the Ancient Furnace! Jennifer was incensed at herself for not considering the possibility.

Her aim was true. Unprepared for her physical assault, Otto took her full force in the mandibles and cried out as she toppled him from his perch. In a clutter of wings and legs, they fell off the pillar together and into the murky stream below.

The dirty water was deeper than it looked. Jennifer could barely see the arachnid body that pushed against her, but she did not care. This thing had kidnapped and hurt her father, stolen her blood, tried to put her in a coma, nearly killed the son who had tried to save her, and now was taking shots at her best friend. Enough was enough.

With her wings and claws occupied with his eight squirming appendages, she used the only weapon left—her mouth. Her jaws snapped out once, twice, three times. On the third try, her teeth closed on the spider's head. She could feel her fangs sink into a gelatinous mass—an eye?—and heard Otto's gurgled scream. Knowing his mandibles were open inside of her jaws, she let loose with the fiercest underwater whistle she could manage.

Ten rings of fire raged through the water, boiling it as they passed through Otto's mandibles and into his tortured head. He wasn't pushing anymore—he was panicking.

She felt his body lift up out of the water in a mighty jump and hung on. They burst out of the water together and vaulted high into the air before landing squarely on the slippery stones in a heap, side by side, with a grunt.

Before Jennifer could even gather herself, there was a silver flash, a soft *ploonk*, and the clink of metal against stone.

She looked up. The beaststalker had been waiting. Her sword pierced Otto's abdomen about two inches from Jennifer's own gray belly. The blade had come down with such force, the point was stuck into the stone beneath the gigantic body. Once again, Jennifer thought of the pinned butterflies in science class.

Getting up, she saw the armored shape slump with exhaustion against the fallen enemy. "Susan, you okay?"

Otto's croaking voice caught their attention. He spat his words through torn and burnt mandibles. Dark blood pooled under the junction between his reddish yellow abdomen and black head.

"You fools," he grated. "You've got no idea what's coming. *This is not over.*"

"It is for you," Jennifer replied. She grasped the hilt of the beaststalker's sword with a trembling wing claw, yanked it out of his abdomen, and ran it through his head.

He shuddered, and then his legs curled in.

"Give me that!" The beaststalker's fury as she snatched the sword away surprised Jennifer. Without another word, she brushed Jennifer aside, leapt over the stream, and stormed over to where Jonathan and Skip sat huddled against the wall. After a brief check of Jonathan's burn (it

covered his arm, but wasn't serious), she lifted the unconscious Skip onto her shoulder, blanket and all, and carried him back to the opposite side of the room, jumping over the stream once more as if she carried nothing at all.

Jennifer noticed Geddy sputtering on the bricks edging the stream. She had forgotten he was on her back throughout the entire fight! With a quiet word of comfort, she gently picked him up and laid him on her shoulder.

"Hey, wait up!"

Everyone else was already halfway down one of the rough-hewn tunnels that carried water into the junction room. There was a narrow ledge on either side of the stream, and before long they were all in the utility room Jennifer and Skip had first entered. While the other two carried Skip up the ladder, Jennifer simply flew up the shaft until the cool air, sunlight, and scent of lilacs were on her face.

Landing on the field by the culvert and looking upon the edge of a town she'd never thought she'd see again, Jennifer smiled. But before there was time to enjoy their escape, the beaststalker wheeled around and was upon her.

"Young lady, you are in a heap of trouble! What kind of idiot rushes headlong into an enemy lair with no plan, no confirmation of what she's even facing, no backup strategy? You live in a world beyond all conceivable luck that your damn gecko knew enough to follow you to your cell and then come back for help—he obviously makes a smarter lizard than you do! Hey! Are you even listening to me?"

The beaststalker could have been forgiven for not being sure: Jennifer's expression was lost somewhere between stupefaction and discovery. The voice was clearer to Jennifer now . . . all too clear. A woman, yes—but this wasn't

Susan at all. With a move even faster than the beaststalker could track, she brought her wing claw up and lifted the helm off.

"Mom?!?"

Elizabeth Georges-Scales shook her honey blonde hair out. Her emerald eyes were smoldering with anger and laced with tears. *"Jennifer Caroline Scales, do you have any idea how abysmally stupid you are?!?!"*

Jennifer dropped the helm and hugged her mother. She didn't let go until she had morphed back into the beaststalker's daughter.

CHAPTER 16

Crescent Valley

The ordeal in Otto's lair, combined with her unusual morph and the shock of discovering what her mother was, exhausted Jennifer. She went to sleep that evening and didn't even stir through the next day.

By the time she woke up, it was sunrise. To her great surprise, she didn't want to get out of bed even then—because Skip was sitting right at her bedside, with a grin on his face. Geddy was curled up on the boy's left shoulder, sleeping.

"Skip, I'm not dressed! What're you doing in here?"

He pretended to cover his eyes. "Your dad let me in."

"But you were almost dead!"

"I'm a fast healer. Being what I am—or will be, someday—helped, of course. My father's poison would have done way more damage to *you*. The folks at the hospital couldn't believe how I healed either, but they couldn't force me to stay. I feel fine, even if there is a nasty scar." He pulled up his shirt and showed her the angry red diagonal across his bare chest. It sported thirty or forty stitches already starting to fall out.

"Huh. So you say my father let you in? He's not exactly one to invite boys into my bedroom."

"Maybe he trusts me after what happened—or he realized I'd just use the trellis up to your window anyway. He definitely likes me more than your mother does—she's been just outside the entire time I've been here, waiting for me to suck your blood or spin a web or something."

"You're damn right!" Elizabeth popped open the bedroom door without knocking. Geddy started on Skip's shoulder, opened an eye, and licked it.

"All right, buster, you wanted to be here when she woke up. She's awake. Now beat it."

"It's okay, Mom," Jennifer insisted, pulling her bed sheets as tightly around her neck as she could. "If he wants to talk, I don't mind."

"Hmmph." Perhaps Elizabeth was relieved to see her daughter awake, or perhaps she remembered Skip's father and how he died. Her face softened and she retreated without argument, leaving the door open. They heard her footsteps fade down the hall and stairs.

Skip's easy grin wavered as he looked at Jennifer again. "Jennifer, I'm so sorry. I would never have . . . I mean, my dad told me what you were, and I thought—"

"You don't have to explain," Jennifer interrupted. "I mean, I was really mad, but what you did in that cell . . . well, you came through when it counted. As far as I'm concerned, that makes up for . . . for other stuff. Thanks."

His shoulders slumped with relief. "I was so afraid you'd never want anything to do with me again. In fact, I was surprised you didn't leave me on the floor of that cell. Dad was wrong about you. All of you. I won't forget that."

"Skip, you know that . . . um . . . your dad . . . ?"

"Yeah, I know." He breathed deeply. "He's dead. My aunt Tavia told me while I was at the hospital. She says they found him with stab and bite wounds. I went back down in the sewers yesterday night. They had taken his body, but there was still a bunch of dead snakes and spiders." There was a meaningful pause. "I don't suppose you know anything more?"

Jennifer could see now that Skip was not just here to apologize. But she could not blame him—his father was dead, for good or bad, and he wanted to know how.

"I understand why you're asking," she answered carefully. "And I'm sure *you* understand if I'm not quite ready to betray the person who rescued me. Any more than I'd betray you."

Skip nodded sadly. "Okay. I won't ask anymore. I just wish Dad . . . I wish Mom . . ." He stared past her bed, out the window for several seconds. "I don't know *what* I wish."

He suddenly got up and rubbed his eyes, making Geddy hop onto her pillow and curl up there. Gently touching her wrist, he pressed something into her palm. "I also went back for this. I meant what I said the first time. Er . . . if you and I are okay, Jennifer, I gotta go. I'm not used to crying in front of girls I really like. Cool?"

"Cool." She waved as he left. Then she looked down at her hand. The necklace of the Moon of Falling Leaves was in her hand. Her fingers closed around it.

Later that day, as afternoon turned into evening, Jennifer caught her mother on her way out of the house. "Where're you going?" she asked. It made her nervous to see any member of her family leaving.

Elizabeth turned and blinked at her daughter. "I'm going to get materials for you to train. You have another part of your heritage to develop, now."

"Mom . . ." Jennifer thought back to the beginning of the school year. "That kick at the championship soccer game. The way I can jump. That's not the dragon in me, is it?"

After looking conspiratorially around the foyer, her mother sighed. "Your father sucks at soccer. Even when he was in college, he couldn't kick a beach ball into the ocean."

She straightened. "This summer, you're going to learn what it means to be a beaststalker. It's not going to be easy. Are you up for it?"

Jennifer's gray eyes sparkled. "I can keep up with you, old woman."

Her mother's voice was without humor. "No, you can't. But you'll figure that out soon enough."

"Mom? I'm sorry for what I said to you, outside the Blacktooths's. About being a coward."

"Forgiven and forgotten." Elizabeth gave her an inscrutable look. "And what I said ended up being true, anyway: Nothing could stop the Scales girls, when we worked together."

As she walked out the door, she turned back one last time. "Don't forget to feed that dorky lizard of yours. He did, after all, save your life."

After feeding Geddy an extra calcium-coated cricket, Jennifer found her father resting in dragon shape by the living room sofa. His burns had largely healed upon that morning's morph. She scrunched up on the floor next to him and laid her head down on his side. Her hair splayed out over his wing—there were very few blonde strands left, she noticed, while twirling silver through her fingers.

Geddy scurried along the carpet toward them. Phoebe intercepted the tiny lizard and gave him such an enthusiastic sniff, she knocked him head over tail.

"Thanks for letting Skip in, Dad."

"Sure. Susan's been by a couple times, too, but she had to go home. I imagine she'll visit again tonight. Skip insisted that he stay until you woke up. I had a sneaking feeling he wouldn't do anything to hurt you, at least not anymore." There was a wry smile in his voice.

"Why haven't I morphed yet?"

"I should think the answer is obvious by now," he replied. "You apparently don't want to, at the moment. Being the Ancient Furnace gives you the power to change back and forth at will."

She sighed contentedly. "I'm glad I can choose. Being a mythical figure has its perks, I guess!"

"I guess! You're doubtless the only thousand-year legend with a curfew."

"Curfew, schmurfew! Hey, um, so we don't need to move, right? And I can go to school without playing sick?"

"That's right. Your grandfather and I are still trying to piece together the information we have, but best we can tell, as long as you don't put off morphing for weeks and weeks, you should be able to choose when and why it happens. For a while, though, you'll want to watch your temper . . . that looks like a trigger."

"Speaking of temper—is Mom okay? I can't tell if she's still angry with me."

"She's furious with you, Jennifer. And relieved beyond belief. And full of love for you. So am I, on all counts. Would you have it any other way?"

"I guess not. I'm sorry I freaked you both out. I don't know what I was thinking."

"I have a general idea. I can't say for sure that I wouldn't have been just as hasty to find you, if our positions had been reversed. Your mother always was the calm, collected one."

Jennifer tried to think of how to ask the next question. "Does that come from being a beaststalker?"

"If you're asking me if all beaststalkers are calm and collected, then I only have to point you to the Blacktooths for proof that they are not. Most beaststalkers crave conflict. Your mother, as you already know, does not."

Jennifer sighed inwardly—thinking of the Blacktooths made her think of Eddie. She supposed he wouldn't stop by to see if she was okay, like Skip and Susan had. Things would never be the same between them again. That hurt.

Her father continued. "But if you're *really* asking me if you've got as much beaststalker in you as dragon—and I think you are—then I'll answer your question with a question. Where do you think that owl came from, the first time you tried lizard-calling with Ned?"

She raised her head. "That wasn't a mistake?"

"Beaststalkers practice for years before they can summon birds of prey. Remember the golden eagles we saw on the lake, when you first learned how to fly? Or the ones that followed you to the sewer?"

"So it *was* the same birds! Those were Mom's? She can call *eagles*?"

"She calls the same pair every time. It's a good thing she had them, too—those led her as far as the sewer entrance, and then Geddy did the rest."

"That's so cool! *Eagles.* Jeez. How come she never told me what she is, or what she could do?"

"How come you never asked?"

"Touché." She put her head back on his wing. "So anyway, she told me I'm going to get to learn to do all the cool stuff she can do! I really want to do that wicked light and sound show."

His forked tongue flickered at her. "Now, don't give up learning your dragon skills! There's more than the few you've learned so far—and you could improve on some of those, too." He winked.

"Improve on an army of black mambas? I don't think so. And I'll have you know my camouflage is going to get me out of your so-called curfew a million times."

"You don't even come close to *my* camouflage."

"Oh, no?"

"Well, you tell me. Did you see me in your bedroom while you were talking to Skip?"

She gasped. "You . . ."

His scaled stomach heaved with a chuckle. "I can do a mean dirty laundry pattern, let me tell you . . ."

"That was an invasion of my privacy!" She tried to be irritated, but curiosity got the better of her. "How did you do both my plaid and striped sweaters, at once?"

"You're right, it was an invasion of your privacy. And I'm sorry. But it was the only way I could get your mother to promise not to stand behind Skip's shoulder the entire time he was there. I won't do it again."

The mention of Skip made Jennifer pensive again. "He doesn't know who killed his dad."

"I know. He and I had a short talk before I let him upstairs. He's not stupid—he's sure you were involved in your own escape—but I think he's shown maturity in waiting for all the facts to come in before he judges. Of course, his aunt and others may not feel the same way. So you did well to answer him as you did. As you can imagine, your mother's involvement *must* remain secret. After all, as your grandfather told you—no dragon has ever *reported* seeing a beaststalker for years!" His eyes twinkled at that.

"What happened between Skip's mother and you that got Otto Saltin so angry?"

Jonathan sighed. "I'll tell you the same thing I told Skip. It's not the whole story, but it will do for now. I knew Dianna Wilson, long before she married Otto. And I knew what she was, just like she knew what I was. But we were the best of friends.

"Otto put an end to that friendship. I don't know that you need to know much more than that, just yet. Anyway, Skip tells me they didn't last long together, and he grew up with his mother, journeying around the world."

"I remember him talking about western Africa, and Australia, and South America," Jennifer recalled, fingering her necklace.

"Meanwhile, Otto has remained close by. He led the werachnids at Eveningstar, and he must have moved secretly to Winoka a few years after we did to begin building his lair and setting his plans for you. He would need to wait until you got old enough to morph, as he said. Then he would be sure of what you were, and have your blood at full potency.

"Skip coming to him this year was an unexpected gift—a way for him to lure you. Just before Christmas,

Otto and I accidentally ran into each other at a town meeting. By then, his plan for you must already have been in motion. I feel foolish for not putting it all together. If I had just gone with you that one time to the mall, I would have seen who Skip's father really was!"

Jennifer couldn't believe her father. "Dad, Skip kept his mother's name—there are dozens of Wilsons in every town in this state. How on earth would you make a connection like that?"

"It's a father's job to pry and connect," he answered. "From now on I do a complete checkup on every friend—especially every boy—you bring into this house."

"Great." To her surprise, Jennifer didn't feel as sarcastic as she sounded. She got more comfortable. "I like that you were friends with one of them."

"I like that you're friends with one yourself." He paused. "It won't be easy, Jennifer. And it may not end well, after all. But the friends who stay with you through changes are worth the effort. They are a rare kind."

"Especially the ones who take a bit of poison in the gut for you."

"Yes, you're lucky to know one of those!"

"And *you're* lucky Mom and I are both freaks. If we were normal people, you'd have been in trouble down there."

His wing claw combed her silver hair. "If you were normal, Jennifer, you wouldn't be a Scales."

"Spoken like a true freak. Does everyone talk like you in Crescent Valley, wherever that is?"

His head perked up. "Come with me and find out!"

The suddenness of the proposal shocked her. "Crescent Valley? But I thought—you said I couldn't—I've only—are there newolves there?"

"Lots," he chuckled. "I think you're ready, now. And given who you are, I think I can convince the Elder Council to agree. Jennifer, you won't believe what you're about to see. This world is going to blow you away."

"Okay, sounds great! But wait—what about Mom?"

"We'll leave her a message. She'll understand. We've got to get moving, though—the moonlight won't be on the water for long."

Moonlight on the water. He had mentioned that before, but . . . "But Mom and I were going to start beaststalker training!"

His silver eyes flashed as he smiled urgently and held out a wing. "Be a beaststalker tomorrow. Today be a dragon, and nothing else, one last time."

She smiled back, and by the time she grabbed his wing, it was with a wing of her own. Then they were out the door together, and under the twilit crescent moon. Jennifer had no idea what was coming next.

The thought pleased her.

THE ULTIMATE IN FANTASY!

From magical tales of distant worlds to stories of those with abilities beyond the ordinary, Ace and Roc have everything you need to stretch your imagination to its limits.

Marion Zimmer Bradley/Diana Paxon

Guy Gavriel Kaye

Dennis McKiernan

Patricia McKillip

Robin McKinley

Sharon Shinn

Katherine Kurtz

Barb and J. C. Hendees

Elizabeth Bear

T. A. Barron

Brian Jacques

Robert Asprin

penguin.com